South Sea Adventure

Roger looked doubtfully at his brother. Hal did not move. But both of them came suddenly to life when the gun roared. Kaggs fired two shots, one of them barely missing Hal and the other coming within a hair's breadth of Roger.

Hal and Roger, sailing the Pacific, find themselves in danger often enough in their search for sea creatures as deadly as octopuses and giant squid. But it takes all their courage and strength to survive after the villain Kaggs leaves them marooned on an uninhabited coral reef with no food or water.

About the author

Willard Price was born in Peterborough, Ontario
Canada, in 1887. After university he travelled a
great deal and went to seventy-seven countries;
he spent time in Europe, Africa, South America
and China, and lived for six years in Japan.
Many of his forays abroad were expeditions on
behalf of the American Museum of Natural
History and the National Geographic Society.
He died in 1983.

Also by Willard Price
and available in Knight Books:

Amazon Adventure
Underwater Adventure
Elephant Adventure
Gorilla Adventure
Volcano Adventure
Diving Adventure
Cannibal Adventure
Whale Adventure
African Adventure
Safari Adventure
Lion Adventure
Tiger Adventure
Arctic Adventure

South Sea Adventure

Willard Price

*Illustrated from drawings
by Pat Marriott*

KNIGHT BOOKS
Hodder and Stoughton

For KEN

Printed and bound in Great Britain for Hodder and Stoughton Paperbacks, a division of Hodder and Stoughton Ltd., Mill Road, Dunton Green, Sevenoaks, Kent TN13 2YA. (Editorial Office: 47 Bedford Square, London WC1B 3DP) by Richard Clay Ltd., Bungay, Suffolk.

ISBN 0-340-03826-8

Contents

1 Bring them back alive 7

2 The danger of knowing too much 11

3 The downhill run 17

4 Mysteries of the deep 24

5 The giant sea bat 28

6 Coral atoll 36

7 Argument with an octopus 43

8 Hurricane 54

9 Into the lost world 66

10 The pearl trader 71

11 The mysterious passenger 80

12 To the secret atoll 83

13 Pearl lagoon 92

14 Desert island 104

15 The sharkskin house 116

16 The castaways eat 124

17 The giant with ten arms 133

18 The pearl divers 141

19 The raft 147

20 Disaster in the waterspout 156

21 The wreck of the 'Hope' 168

22 Rescue and rest 179

23 Towards new adventures 185

1 | Bring them back alive

JOHN HUNT put down the phone. He sat for a moment, thinking, tapping his pencil nervously on his desk.

The roar of lions, scream of hyenas, cough of jaguars, came in the open window – sounds strange to hear within an hour's journey of New York. They were nothing new to the man at the desk. He was an animal collector. It was his business to bring them back alive from the ends of the earth, keep them in his animal farm until called for, then sell them to zoos, menageries, circuses, motion-picture companies – anyone who might have use for any sort of wild creature from an African elephant to a titmouse.

But he had never had so strange a request as the one that had just come over the phone.

'Hal!' he called. 'Come in – and bring Roger with you.'

When his sons entered, they found him studying a wall map of the Pacific. He turned to them.

'Well, boys,' he said as casually as if he were merely proposing an afternoon's picnic, 'how soon can you take off for the South Seas?'

'Dad, you don't mean it!' exploded thirteen-year-old Roger.

His big brother, Hal, with the calm of a young man about to enter the university, managed to suppress his excitement. Hal was not going to let a little thing like the South Seas make him act like a juvenile.

After all, wasn't he an experienced animal man? He and his kid brother had just come back from an animal hunt in the Amazon jungle – a story already told in the book *Amazon Adventure*. They had brought home living specimens of the jaguar, ant bear, vampire bat, anaconda, boa-constrictor, sloth, and tapir. Surely their father could not have in mind any creature of the South Seas that would be stranger or more difficult to capture than these.

John Hunt looked at his sons proudly. Roger was still too young and too full of mischief to make a first-rate animal man; but Hal was a steady fellow. He was larger and stronger than his father. Leaving him in charge of an expedition in the Amazon wilds had been a risky experiment – but it had paid off. He could be trusted now with a bigger job.

'You know I promised you a trip to the South Seas if you made a success of the Amazon project. I didn't expect it would come so soon. But I've just had an urgent call – from Henry Bassin. You've heard his name.'

'He made a fortune in steel,' remembered Hal. 'What does he want with animals?'

'He's building a private aquarium on his estate. He says he wants the strangest things from the Seven Seas. He has one big pool reserved for – what do you think?'

'Sea lions,' said Hal contemptuously.

'No. A giant octopus.'

Hal forgot his poise. 'Not one of those monsters thirty

feet across! How could we ever get it? He's asking the impossible.'

'But that's not all,' went on his father, consulting a pad on which he had pencilled his notes. 'He wants a tiger shark, a flying gurnard, a grampus, a sea lizard, a dugong, a conger-eel, one of those huge clams that are fond of catching divers between their jaws, a manta or sea bat . . .'

'Why, they grow big enough to sink a boat,' said Hal in dismay. 'How . . .'

'A sea centipede,' continued Hunt, 'a sawfish, and a swordfish, and a giant squid . . . yes,' he added, enjoying the startled expression on Hal's face, 'the squid that grows tentacles up to forty feet long, has suction cups as big as plates, and an eye fifteen inches across . . . the one that has earned for itself the pleasant name of "nightmare of the Pacific".'

'But how would we ever get such big specimens home?'

'You'll charter a schooner with tanks big enough for two or three such specimens at a time. These can be transferred to freighters and shipped home.'

'Oh, boy!' Roger began to dance. 'We'll sail our own schooner?'

'Nothing elaborate,' warned his father. 'No yacht. Just a fishing boat. You'll fly from here to San Francisco, get a boat there, and take on a crew. Then get to work. Of course Bassin's job is only part of it. You'll collect other specimens, large and small that are in demand by public aquariums. Perhaps I'll send you more assignments as you go along. It depends on your performance. You've been wanting to skip a year of school because you're both too young for your classes. That may be a good idea. I'll try to give you more education in a year than you could get in a classroom. There are jobs in Japan, Alaska, Africa, waiting to be done. Whether you get to do them depends upon you '

He looked wistfully out of the window.

'I wish I could go with you – but there's too much here to

attend to. Besides,' he sighed, 'I'm afraid I'm getting too old for that sort of rough-and-tumble.'

The eagerness of the boys as contrasted with the weariness of the older man showed that it was exactly the idea of rough-and-tumble that appealed to them.

'How soon can we get off?' asked Hal.

'Just as soon as you can pack and get seats in a plane. By the way – before you leave, drop around to see Professor Stuyvesant. He asked me to let him know next time I sent anybody down Pacific way. He has a project out there that he wants somebody to look in on. Something to do with pearls.'

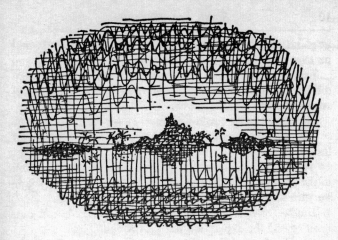

2 | The danger of knowing too much

'Close the door,' said the professor. 'We must not be overheard.'

Hal closed the door and resumed his seat beside Roger at the scientist's desk. Professor Stuyvesant glanced about the room as if he feared that even the walls might have ears. They had – but all the ears were deaf. The famous zoologist was surrounded by friends he could trust not to listen and not to talk. Some were stuffed and some were pickled, but they were all alike in one way – they were all thoroughly dead. Auks, penguins, terns, moonfish, peacock fish, sea bass, tuna, mullet, hermit crabs, jellyfish, puffers, porpoises, and porcupine fish stood in rows on shelves that lined the walls from floor to ceiling.

Dr Richard Stuyvesant was a world authority on sea life. He conducted an advanced course in the university and was executive secretary of the National Oceanographic Institute. He knew the oceans. He knew fish. His researches in the employ of great commercial fishing interests of America,

England, and Norway had brought him such rewards that he had been able to buy this big gloomy old mansion and convert it into a great laboratory. In nearly every room there were tanks and a fish-breeding experiment of one sort or another was going on.

The grey-haired professor lowered his head so that he could peer at his visitors sharply through the upper part of his trifocals.

'Your father tells me that you are making an expedition to the Pacific,' he said, and smiled. 'You seem rather young for such a responsibility.'

'But we have had some experience,' said Hal, and outlined briefly the expedition to the Amazon.

'Well,' reflected the scientist, 'I have known your father for many years and have the utmost confidence in him – and so must have confidence in you too. I must say at the start that this matter is highly confidential. And rather dangerous too. You see, there's a valuable secret involved. Twice my life has been threatened if I did not divulge this secret. Three times this room has been entered by unknown persons at night and my files ransacked. They didn't find what they wanted – because it's not written down. It's no place but here,' and he tapped his forehead.

'To do the errand I have in mind,' went on the professor, 'you will have to know this secret. But if you know it, you are likely to be annoyed as I have been by the person or persons who are trying to steal this information. Perhaps you would rather not run this risk?' He looked inquiringly at Hal.

'Tell us more about the project,' Hal suggested.

The professor fished a map out of a drawer and opened it on the desk. Roger felt electric sparks move along his spine. Was this a pirate chart of buried treasure of the sort he had read about in tales of roving swashbucklers and Spanish galleons?

But then he saw it was only a National Geographic map

of the western Pacific from Hawaii to Taiwan. It was a big map and spattered with myriads of islands never shown on smaller maps.

Hawaii, Tahiti, Samoa, Fiji, were familiar names. But the professor's pencil circled an area littered with islands bearing such names as Ponape, Truk, Yap, Olol, Losap, Pakin, Pingelap, and many others as peculiar.

'This is the blind spot of the Pacific,' said the professor. 'There are twenty-five hundred nearly unknown islands in this area. For thirty years they constituted the Japanese mandate and Japan jealously kept foreign ships out of these seas. During World War II a few, a very few, of these islands were the scene of fighting but most of them were by-passed by Allied ships on their way to Japan. Now all the islands of what was the Japanese mandate are a trusteeship placed by the United Nations under control of the United States – and on some of the islands you will find American naval stations. The boys of the navy have a pretty lonesome time out there. It's almost like a lost world.

'Now, the good thing about this lost world so far as you and I are concerned, is that it is the best place in the Pacific to collect marine specimens and it also happens to be the scene of my pearl farm.'

'Pearls!' exclaimed Roger under his breath.

Dr Stuyvesant put the point of his pencil on the island named Ponape. 'North of this island – I won't say just how far – there is a small uninhabited atoll. It is too small to show on this map and since it is quite off the paths of ocean travel, it does not even appear on nautical charts. I have chosen to call it Pearl Lagoon. I am conducting an experiment in that lagoon.

'The most beautiful pearls in the world are produced in the Persian Gulf. Five years ago I collected twenty thousand Persian Gulf oysters and transported them under natural conditions of habitat to my Pearl Lagoon. I brought also large quantities of the organisms that are the customary food of these oysters. I am trying to reproduce the Persian Gulf in Pearl Lagoon and I hope to show that it is possible to raise pearls in the American Trusteeship, as well as in adjacent British waters, equal to the finest to be found anywhere.

'It is time to see how my experiment is working out. I can't go myself, and I can't afford to send someone for that purpose alone. But perhaps in the course of your other duties you could stop by at Pearl Lagoon and get me some specimens from my oyster beds. Of course I'll take care of any expense involved in this side trip.'

'It sounds like a mighty interesting assignment,' said Hal. 'Naturally we'd have to know the exact location of Pearl Lagoon.'

'Exactly. And that is the secret.' He glanced about. Then he leaned forward and fixed Hal with his penetrating gaze. 'Do you have a curious feeling that we are being over-heard?'

'Not particularly,' smiled Hal.

The professor smiled back and shrugged his shoulders. 'I'm probably just imagining things. It's all this trouble – threatening letters – intruders at night. And yet I wouldn't be at all surprised if there were a dictograph planted some-where in this room, and someone listening at the other end of the wire. I've searched, but couldn't find a thing.

'But I'm sure that all I have told you so far is already known to my enemies. And what I'm about to tell you now they won't hear.'

He tore a slip of paper from a pad and wrote on it: N. Lat. 11.34. E. Long. 158.12.

He pushed the paper before the boys.

'This is the first time these figures have been written down and I hope the last time. I suggest you commit them to memory. They are the bearings of Pearl Lagoon. You must never write them down and never speak them to any-one.'

The boys concentrated on the task of memorizing the bearings – North Latitude 11 degrees 34 minutes, East Longitude 158 degrees 12 minutes.

When the professor was satisfied that the lesson had been learned he turned over the slip and drew an irregular outline. 'The lagoon,' he said. 'This direction is north. The oyster bed is here,' and he placed the point of his pencil on a cove in the north-east corner of the lagoon.

Again he paused to let this information take root in the boys' minds.

Then he struck a match and burned the paper to a crisp. He placed the charred remains between his palms and rubbed them until there was nothing left but fine ash.

As the boys came out of the house to regain their father's car in which they had made the trip to the city, Hal noticed a man come hurriedly from the next house. The man's face could not be seen and there was nothing noticeable about him except the slight hunch of his back. He got into a black sedan.

Hal would not have noticed these details if he had not been keyed up by the curious interview of the last half-hour with its air of secrecy and suspicion.

He drove out to the animal farm. As he entered the home driveway he saw a black sedan go by and continue down the highway.

Hal felt a sudden impulse to give chase. He began to whirl his car about.

'Hey, what's the idea?' Roger protested.

Hal laughed, straightened out, and drove on to the house. He told himself that he was letting his imagination run away with him. Why should he suppose that the car he had just seen was the same as the one he had noticed in town? The world was full of black sedans.

And yet, suppose someone had seen them go into the scientist's house and come out again. Suppose he had even heard their conversation. Suppose the professor's enemy was now their enemy too. Suppose that by following them to the Hunt Animal Farm he now knew where they lived and that their name was Hunt. What would his next move be?

'Suppose I quit supposing,' said Hal severely to himself and tried to dismiss the subject from his mind.

3 | The downhill run

'How she scoons!' cried Roger as the fishing schooner, *Lively Lady*, sped out of San Francisco Bay between the pillars of Golden Gate Bridge and into the Pacific on the first lap of her 'downhill run' to the South Seas.

For Roger recalled the story that someone had exclaimed, 'How she scoons!' when the first craft of this sort put to sea. The owner had replied, 'A scooner let her be.' And from that time on this type of vessel was known as a scooner or schooner, from the old verb scoon, meaning to skip or skim.

And certainly the ship the boys had chartered seemed to skip and skim now as she flew wing-and-wing before the wind.

She had been built for speed to get a tuna catch to port before her rivals. She carried the fastest sail in the world, the triangular Marconi sail, instead of the gaff mainsail usually seen on schooners. This triangle of sail put her in a class with racing yachts, and indeed she had competed successfully more than once in the annual cup races.

But she was different in other ways from the ordinary schooner. Between the two masts, in place of the usual foresail, she carried two staysails, while forward of the foremast billowed a giant jib.

There was an auxiliary engine but it was only to help the ship through narrow passages when the wind failed. Given a fair wind, her sails could push her along at twice the speed that could be wrung out of her engine. Right now she was doing seventeen knots with ease.

Hal and Roger strode the deck with mighty pride. Temporarily at least she was their ship although the money with which they had chartered her came from John Hunt and his

wealthy client and she still carried her real owner on board, Captain Ike Flint.

He served as skipper, for the boys as yet knew too little about sailing to handle a sixty-foot ship. The skipper's crew consisted of two brawny young seamen, one of them a rough, hard-bitten character nicknamed Crab who refused to be bothered with a real name, and the other a handsome brown giant named Omo, a native of the South Sea isle of Raiatea. He had come to San Francisco as a hand on a trading ship, had been bewildered by the rush of American life, and was now well content to be heading back towards the Polynesian islands.

Captain Ike and his men would sleep in a snug cabin under the forward deck. Hal and Roger would occupy a still snugger cabin aft. Space had been stolen from it to afford more room for the huge specimen tanks that had been installed amidships. These filled the hold between the two cabins.

It was not possible to use one giant tank for all specimens, for the big creatures would devour the little ones. They must be kept separate. And that meant many tanks, large and small. These various aquariums were covered with removable lids. Even when these covers were battened down air was admitted to each tank by a valve in the lid so devised that while it would allow air to go in it would not permit water to come out even in the roughest weather.

In a tiny galley was a Primus stove and a stock of food. A storeroom was stuffed with supplies including equipment needed for gathering specimens, seines, gill nets, tow nets, scoop nets, poles and lines, and harpoons.

High on the crosstrees of the mainmast was a platform that would serve as a crow's-nest where a lookout might sit and watch the sea for game.

Out ahead of the ship on the tip of her bowsprit was a pulpit – the sort in which a fisherman stands, harpoon in hand, watching for swordfish. It was thrilling to stand here with nothing but the sky above and the rushing sea beneath.

From this point you could look straight down into water still undisturbed by the ship. If anything interesting came along you were in a position to get a preview of it.

And who could tell what discoveries the two young explorers might make? The professor had said, 'Probably more than half of the living things of the Pacific are still unknown to science.'

This enormous ocean, eleven thousand miles across at its widest part, averaging three miles deep and at some points six times as deep as the Grand Canyon, sprinkled with tens of thousands of islands of which only three thousand have yet been named – what secrets it must still hold locked in its mighty deeps.

Captain Ike stood at the wheel. His small blue eyes, as sharp as the eyes of a fox, peered out of a brown leather face at the wavering needle of the compass in the binnacle before him. He held the ship to a course south-west by south.

'With luck,' he said, 'we could slide downhill all the way to Ponape.'

'Why do they call this the downhill run?' asked Hal.

'Because we're in the path of the trades. That doesn't mean much to a steamer but it's everything to a sailing ship. With the trade winds behind us we'll make fast time. O' course here in the horse latitudes they're a bit temperamental, but when we get past Hawaii they ought to be mighty steady – barring accidents.'

'What accidents?'

'Hurricanes. They can spoil the best of plans.'

'Is this the season for them?'

'It is. But no telling. We might be lucky. Anyway,' and he gave Hal a sharp glance, 'what you're after is worth the trouble.'

Hal was suddenly suspicious. Was the captain fishing for

information? Or did he already know more than he was supposed to know? He had been told only that they were after marine specimens. No mention had been made of pearls.

Hal turned away and walked the deck. The buoyant exhilaration he had felt as the ship raced before the wind was dulled by worry.

He had almost ceased to think of the menace that had threatened the expedition before it left home. There had been no sign that anyone had shadowed them at the airfield or on the plane or during the days in San Francisco. When they sailed out into the great freedom of the Pacific he felt that all evil plots had been left behind and that there was nothing ahead but delightful adventure.

Now he wondered about Captain Ike. He wondered about the rough fellow named Crab. He wondered about Omo – being from the South Seas, might he not have picked up some information about the professor's experiment?

'What's eating you?' demanded Roger, noting his brother's worried look.

Hal laughed. He wouldn't worry Roger with his ill-founded fears. 'Just wondering if we were going to have a change in the weather. See that cloud?'

'It looks as if it meant business,' said Roger, looking up at the black cloud passing above. Presently a few drops fell.

'Rain!' exclaimed Hal. 'That means a bath to me. Here goes to get off some of that sweaty dirt I put on in the city.'

He dashed down into the cabin and came up a few moments later stripped naked, with a cake of soap in his hand.

As the raindrops wet his skin he vigorously soaped himself all over until he was covered with a white lather from head to foot. He waited for the rain to increase in volume and wash him clean.

Instead, the rain ceased abruptly. The black cloud passed over and not another drop was squeezed out of it. Hal stood like a pillar of soap, waiting patiently, and considerably embarrassed under the gaze of the captain and crew. He consoled himself with the thought that there were no ladies on board and none within dozens of miles.

But his mischievous younger brother, much amused, had a sudden flash of inspiration. He went down to the storeroom and opened the slop chest. He had already seen a woman's dress and hat in this chest and when he had asked about them the captain had explained that his wife sometimes accompanied him on his voyages.

Roger hastily slipped the dress on over his shirt and slacks. It was big enough for a couple of boys his size. The hat was fortunately very large and droopy, effectively concealing most of his face.

Hal knew that Captain Flint's wife often went along but it had been distinctly understood that this time she would stay home. So he was completely stunned when he saw a female figure rise from the cabin companionway and step out on deck.

He looked for a place of hiding and made a move to get behind the mainmast. At the same moment the lady saw him and the sight was too much for her delicate sensibilities. She screamed to high heaven and fell face downward on the deck.

The poor soul, she had fainted! She might even have killed herself striking her head on the deck. Hal forgot his embarrassment. He ran to her aid, soapsuds flying. He lifted the limp form. He pushed back the big hat and looked into the face of Roger who burst into a mighty guffaw in which he was joined by the captain and Crab.

Laughing always made Roger weak. Hal took advantage of that weakness. He draped his impish brother over his soapy knee and administered a sound spanking.

Roger quit laughing. Hal might have known that that

was a sign of more mischief. Only a low rail stood between the deck and the sea. Roger pretended not to have a muscle in his body. But his drooping hands were close to Hal's foot.

Suddenly he clutched the foot, reared up, and heaved his brother into the ocean.

'Enough of that nonsense,' bawled the captain as he threw the wheel hard over and smartly brought the ship about. He crawled up on the starboard tack, close-hauled, to where Hal, now quite unsoaped, lazily splashed in the water. As the ship bore up to him, Hal reached for the bobstay that held the bowsprit to the stem, and clambered aboard.

His skin tingled with the shock of the cold water. 'Thanks a million, Roger,' he said. 'That was grand.'

He went down and dressed. The fun with Roger and the cold bath that had ended it had restored his high spirits. If there was any menace waiting at the end of the downhill run he felt he would be a match for it.

4 | Mysteries of the deep

IT was night on deck and there was no lantern near enough to read by. And yet Hal was reading.

His only light was a fish!

Swimming about the small tank between the two boys, it threw out a stronger glow than that of a forty-watt bulb.

'Do you find it in the manual?' asked Roger.

'Yes, here it is. A lantern fish. A good name for it!'

The fish has a row of lights along each side, like the lighted portholes of a steamer. Then there were other lights thickly sprinkled over the back. All these lights burned continuously. But most startling were the tail lights which flashed on and off.

Hal had just spent an hour out ahead of the ship on the tip end of the bowsprit. Standing in the pulpit and hanging onto the curved rail which half-surrounded it, he had watched the scudding sea a few feet below him. When he saw anything interesting, his hand net flashed down and up. It was in one of these strikes that he had caught the lantern fish.

'What do you suppose it wants with all those lights?' asked Roger.

'Well,' explained Hal, 'it's a deep-sea fish. It comes to the surface only at night. During the day it lives away down where it is always dark, night and day. So it needs lanterns to find its way about.'

'But the sun can shine through water,' objected Roger.

'The sunlight only goes down a thousand feet or so. Below that, if you did any deep-sea diving, you would need a lamp. On down to the bottom, a distance of a mile to six miles, there is total darkness – or would be if the fish didn't carry lanterns.'

'But what's the idea of those flashing tail lights?'

'Probably to blind enemies. Just as you would be blinded if I flashed an electric torch in your eyes. When I turned it off you wouldn't be able to see me and I could escape.'

'Pretty smart fish,' marvelled Roger.

Every day a net was towed behind the ship. Sometimes it was a surface net, sometimes a deep-sea trawl which collected specimens from a depth of a quarter-mile or more.

These denizens of the deep Hal had put together in a small aquarium.

'Let's put the lantern fish in with his friends,' suggested Roger.

Hal scooped it up with a small net and transferred it to the deep-sea tank.

Immediately there was wild commotion. The lantern fish was pursued by a slightly larger fish which was also sprinkled with lights. Even its fins were illuminated. From its chin dangled brilliantly lighted whiskers.

'Its name is star-eater,' said Hal.

'It sure looks as if it had eaten plenty of stars,' said Roger, following the movements of the star-spangled fish, 'and it will eat some more if it can get that lantern fish.'

Suddenly the lantern fish flashed its blinding tail lights. The confused star-eater stopped and its quarry escaped to hide in a far corner of the tank.

Some of the fish gave out a green light, some yellow, some red. One carried what looked like a small electric bulb suspended in front of its face.

But one had no lights. Hal found its description in his manual. It was blind, therefore it could not use lights to see where it was going. Instead, it was like a blind man walking down the street and tapping with his cane ahead of him. Only in this case there were about twenty canes – long feelers that spread out in every direction like reaching fingers. With these the fish could avoid bumping into unpleasant neighbours, and find its food.

But some of the specimens were not in the manual. Hal wrote descriptions of these and made careful drawings. Perhaps they were new to science. He was their discoverer. Some of them might be named after him.

It seemed a little absurd to Hal and Roger that they should be finding things unknown to the scientists.

'But it could be,' said Hal. 'Last year the Smithsonian Institution made a study of fish near the Bikini atoll. Of four hundred and eighty-one species studied, seventy-nine were new. That's one out of every six. If the same proportion holds here, one out of every six kinds of fish in that tank has never been named or described or had its picture taken until tonight.'

Wham! Something hit the lower staysail just over Hal's head, then fell to the deck. Wham! Wham! Two more.

'Flying-fish!' cried Hal. The tank of luminous fish cast a glow on the staysail. Flying-fish, attracted by the light, were flying on board.

'I'll be catcher!' said Roger, and planted himself in front of the sail. This was as good as baseball. A dark object came hurtling towards him. He caught it neatly and passed it to Omo who had come to gather up the fish. They would be served at breakfast. Flying-fish make fine eating.

Roger caught another, and another. Then a larger object came speeding towards him. It missed his hands and struck him a terrific thump in the stomach. It was as if he had been hit with a sledgehammer. He doubled up, dropped to the deck, and lay still. Hal hastily covered the luminous tank so that no more visitors would be attracted. He leaned over Roger who was beginning to mutter weakly, 'What hit me?'

Planted against Roger's stomach Hal found something that felt like a large rock covered with razor-sharp ridges. He played his torch on it and saw a fish that looked something like a knight in full armour.

'It's a flying gurnard!' he said. 'You might have been

killed.' He remembered stories of sailors at the wheel who had been hit between the eyes by these flying cannonballs and knocked senseless. The knifelike scales had cut through Roger's shirt and drawn blood.

Hal put the flying gurnard into a tank by itself and treated his brother's wounds. When the boy was able to stand they both went to inspect the new catch.

Hal was delighted. 'Mr Bassin will be tickled to get this,' he said. 'It's a circus all by itself. It can swim, it can fly, and it can even walk. Look at it now.'

Sure enough the gurnard was walking about on the bottom of the tank. Two of its fins served as legs. It strolled for a while, then broke into a sudden trot. It ran to a bit of seaweed, turned it over using its fin as a hand, plucked a morsel from under it, and popped it into its mouth.

Roger laughed, holding his hand over his sore stomach. 'What a performer! Mr Bassin will love it. Until it jumps out of the pool and hits the big chief in the pit of the stomach.' He patted his bruised midriff. 'Not that I wish the gentleman any harm but – I'd like to be there when it happens.'

5 | The giant sea bat

'BATS!' cried Roger the next morning from his perch in the crow's-nest. 'I see bats as big as barn doors.'

That sounded silly even to Roger. Bats don't swim. And bats are never as big as barn doors. And yet these were certainly that big and they were swimming along the surface, their great black wings rising and falling.

Roger was official announcer. He spent much of every day in the crow's-nest, watching the sea. His sharp eyes had spotted many interesting specimens. When he saw anything he could call out and the ship would change course if necessary to come up with it. If it proved to be something that Hal wanted, an effort would be made to net it and add it to the collection.

The captain put the wheel over a spoke or two and

headed for the school of black, flapping monsters. Hal
came tumbling up from below with a pair of binoculars. He
could not believe what he saw through them.

'What are they?' he asked Captain Ike.

'Sea bats. Some call 'em devilfish.'

It came back to Hal that this was one of the specimens
his father's important client especially wanted. It was a
manta, a giant ray.

How could they hope to capture one? And would the
biggest tank be big enough to hold it?

The mantas were going around in circles, evidently pur-
suing small fish. As the *Lively Lady* came nearer, all on
board could plainly see what went on. They fixed their
attention especially on one monster close by. It was turning
in a tight circle, one wing above the water and the other
wing under. It was fully twenty feet across from wing-tip to
wing-tip. It was about eighteen feet long from mouth to
tail.

It was chasing a school of mullet.

On each side of its mouth was a great flat flipper or arm.
These arms spread out, gathered in fish, and shovelled them
into the monster's mouth.

And what a mouth! It was four feet wide, big enough to
swallow two men at one gulp.

But Hal knew that the giant ray was not a man-eater. It
preferred fish.

It was extremely dangerous just the same. It had been
known to leap into the air and bring its two-ton weight
down upon a small boat, smashing the boat to kindling
wood and killing its occupants. Its whiplike tail could cut
like a knife. Sometimes instead of falling upon a boat the
giant ray would come up beneath it, lifting it clear out of
the water and then upsetting it. It might then thrash about
among the swimmers, killing or maiming them.

It had no fear of man. Perhaps it was too stupid to fear
him, perhaps it was too confident of its own great strength.

It would sometimes accompany a boat for miles, swimming under it and around it and leaping over it. If the boatmen beat it with their oars, it did not seem to mind. The blows did not disturb it any more than a tap on the ribs would hurt a man.

Once a man had fallen overboard into the great open mouth of the devilfish. The creature evidently didn't like the taste and disgustedly spat him out. The man was unhurt except for a bad scratching from the monster's lower teeth.

The captain brought the ship up into the wind and crawled slowly into the middle of the school. There the ship came to a standstill, sails flapping idly. On every side huge black wings were lifting and dropping. Mantas evidently liked company. They usually travelled in packs. Hal could count twenty-eight of them in this school.

Captain Ike grinned at Hal who looked the picture of bewilderment.

'Well, here we are. What do you want to do?'

'I want to get one of those things alive.'

The captain snorted. 'You'll never do that, son. We could get one of them dead, but not alive. We could harpoon one.'

'That won't do,' said Hal. Then he came out of his trance and began to issue orders. 'Roger and Omo, go below and get the big net. Crab, launch the dinghy. Captain, keep her in stays – we'll be here for some time.'

Captain Ike began to show real worry. 'What are you up to?'

'Going to get in the way of that big fellow. We'll stretch the net between the dinghy and the ship so he'll run into it.'

'You crazy fool...' began the captain, but Hal was not listening.

One lead of the heavy net was made fast to the capstan on the deck of the *Lively Lady*. The net was dropped into the dinghy and Hal, Roger, and Omo let themselves down into the small boat. They rowed away from the ship, letting out the net as they went.

When the net was all out the dinghy was about fifty feet from the ship. The lead of the net was made fast to the mooring bitts in the dinghy.

The circle that the big fellow was making should bring him right into the net. Just what would happen then, nobody dared guess.

Around came the sea bat. He ignored the boat. He looked far larger and more terrifying than he had from the deck of the ship. The upper edge of the net projected from the water.

The devilfish seemed to sense that there was some obstruction ahead of him. But instead of slowing down or swimming to one side he came faster and faster until he was going like a speedboat.

Then he suddenly came clear of the water and soared through the air. He crossed ten feet above the net. He looked like a flying barn door carried away by a cyclone. He reminded Hal of a Northrop flying wing. Then he hit the water on the other side of the net with a sound like the report of a five-inch naval gun.

He came ploughing around again in another circle. His excitement seemed to be transferred to the other mantas and they began to leap out of the water, coming down again with terrific smacks. Some of them turned complete somersaults, their white bellies gleaming in the sun.

Curiosity was bringing them closer to the small boat.

'They're ganging up on us,' cried Roger. Hal began to believe the captain was right. Only a crazy fool could have put himself and two companions in the way of twenty-eight devilfish.

This time it was another manta that approached the net. Instead of leaping over it, it turned sharply away from it and towards the boat. Suddenly finding the boat in its way, it leaped into the air.

The boys were suddenly cut off from the sunshine by the flying cloud. Hal crouched low, fearing the terrible crushing smash of the monster's weight. Roger had a better idea and slipped under a thwart. Omo, belonging to a race that accepts life or death calmly, sat smiling. As the devilfish came down with a terrific crack on the other side of the boat only its razor tail failed to clear the boat and cut a deep gash in the gunwale.

Another manta was examining the boat with great interest. It gave it a crack with one of its powerful armlike fins. If it had struck hard enough it could have smashed the boat. As it was it splintered the top strake on the port side but fortunately the plank was above the waterline and no leak resulted. Then it circled the boat and ran into the net.

'We've got him!' cried Hal.

'If he doesn't back out,' said Roger.

'I think they're just one-way fish. They can't back.'

Certainly the manta was not attempting to go backwards but was trying to bore its way straight through the obstruction. It managed to get one arm through, and then the other. It turned on edge and its tail slipped through the meshes. Once in, it did not come out easily since the tail was covered with sharp spikes that acted as fish-hooks.

'Row!' shouted Hal, and two pairs of oars and a paddle propelled the boat forward and in towards the ship. Thus the net began to close in on the giant ray.

But it was not one to surrender easily. It threshed about violently, churning the sea into whirlpools and sending up geysers of water that promptly soaked the three boatmen. The boat began to settle under the gallons of water that were splashed into it.

It was lucky that the line from the net had been made fast to the mooring bitt, for no man or men could have held it. The tugs on the line jerked the boat here and there, many times nearly upsetting it.

But now the boat was under the counter of the schooner. The captain was leaning over the rail, his eyes popping.

'Quick! Throw me the line.'

Hal pulled the line free of the bitts and heaved it to the captain who caught it deftly and ran to make it fast to the capstan.

Now both ends of the net were secured to the capstan. The sea giant was in a pocket from which there was little chance of escape.

Crab was swinging out the cargo boom. It was hinged to the mainmast and from its seaward end hung a great hook. Hal meshed the hook in the net.

The schooner's engine began to whirr and the net with its writhing contents started upward.

A cheer broke from the boys in the dinghy. But they cheered too soon. In a convulsive struggle the manta flailed out with arms, wing ends, and tail. One of these flying appendages caught the boat amidships and stove it in as if it had been an eggshell.

The boys found themselves in the water and made all haste to swim clear of the churning devilfish. The captain threw out a line and Hal and Roger climbed on board.

They looked back to see that Omo had been struck by the monster's razor-edged tail and was lying in the water, stunned and bleeding. Sharks, instantly attracted by blood, were closing in on him.

Hal drew his knife and was about to leap back into the sea when the captain said, 'Don't do it. You wouldn't have a chance,' and Crab growled, 'Let him sink. He's only a kanaka anyhow.'

It was all Hal needed. Boiling with rage over Crab's callous words, he dived into the blood-tinged sea, not forgetting to take the end of the captain's line with him. This he looped around Omo's chest, meanwhile keeping up a lively splashing and making passes at inquisitive sharks with his knife.

Omo was hauled aboard. Hal fended off sharks until the line came again. Then he lost no time gaining the safety of the deck.

Omo came to life just enough to open one eye and say, 'Thanks!' Then he closed his eye and submitted in silence while Hal dressed the painful wound.

'There goes a good dinghy,' said Captain Ike ruefully, looking at the splinters floating about in the foam whipped up by the whirling mass of fury in the net. 'Hoist away!' he cried, and up, up, went the struggling sea bat. Its teeth and spines cut the net in a dozen places. But the net was made of inch-thick hemp cables and enough of it held until the captive had been brought over the tank and lowered into it.

Hal was glad to see that the tank was just big enough to hold its huge guest. But the visitor did not like its new home and proceeded to splash all the water out of the tank. The pump was turned on and more water poured in. The crew struggled to get the lid on the tank for it seemed quite likely that the manta would leap clear out of its prison and thresh about the decks demolishing spars and rigging.

The lid or hatch was finally locked in place. Then all crowded around the glass porthole to get a look at the prize. It had given up the fight and lay quietly on the bottom of the tank like an immense black blanket. The net was still draped about it.

'How will we get the net out of there?' Roger wanted to know.

Hal had no taste for another bout with his unwilling guest. 'We'll leave him in the net. That way, it will be possible to lift him out of there. We ought to make Honolulu in a couple of days now. We'll tranship him to a cargo steamer bound for home. Then we'll have the tank free in case we want to take on another big passenger.'

'An octopus, maybe?' hoped Roger.

'Maybe. But in the meantime, Roger, you are appointed

chef to Mr Manta. You've got to get enough fish to keep him full and happy.'

'And no dinghy to fish from,' mourned Roger. Then his eyes brightened. 'I think I know how to catch enough fish for his majesty.'

When night came, the fish began to pour on board. For Roger had adjusted a torch so that it threw a bright light on a sail and brought flying-fish by the dozen. When enough had accumulated to make a good meal, Roger and Omo gathered them and dumped them into the tank where they speedily disappeared down the mighty maw of the sea bat.

6 | Coral atoll

'No wonder they call it paradise!' exclaimed Hal as the *Lively Lady* rounded Diamond Head, sailed past the white beach of Waikiki where brown giants stood erect on flying surfboards, glided by lovely groves of palms and flowering trees, and dropped anchor in the harbour of Honolulu.

Hawaii was all the boys had dreamed it should be. But they could stay only long enough to have some tanks built and ship their prizes, including the giant manta, on the cargo steamer *Pacific Star*, bound for New York and London by way of Panama.

Omo did not want them to like Hawaii too much. The islands in the part of the Pacific he called home were quite different.

'Oh, this is all right,' he said with a shrug of his brown shoulders, 'but wait till you see the coral atolls!'

And so, having taken aboard a new dinghy in place of the one destroyed by the too-athletic sea bat, the *Lively Lady* proceeded on her way.

As the ship neared the countless isles and islets of the Marshall archipelago the sea swarmed with life. Dolphins and porpoises raced the schooner for miles, taking time off from the race to indulge in high jumps and broad jumps and play with each other like overgrown puppies. A big sperm whale accompanied the ship for a whole day.

On another day a whale shark, which is truly a shark but as big as a whale, took delight in bumping the ship with its frightfully ugly face. It looked as if its face had been bumped too often. It was twisted and lumpy and had a horrifying expression.

Captain Ike said the whale shark was harmless. But

Roger dreamed about it that night. He woke in terror and turned on his torch, fully expecting to see the whale shark's dreadful face leering at him over the edge of his bunk.

At night the sea gleamed like a sheet of silver. Millions upon millions of plankton, tiny living organisms, glowed with phosphorescent light.

The nets, towed behind, captured many wonderful specimens. When the ship rode into a school of large fish a big trawl net was let down. By this means a bad-tempered conger-eel was captured, and later a swordfish.

But they had trouble with the swordfish. This creature's sword is as deadly as any ever used by the Knights of the Round Table. When the swordfish chooses to attack a boat it can sink it with one thrust of its sword.

The swordfish had not been in the tank for an hour before it pierced its prison wall with its blade and the water ran out. The pump had to be turned on to rid the hold of the water. The swordfish lay gasping on the bottom of the tank.

Prompt action was necessary to save the fish. The hole was hastily patched. But how to prevent the same thing happening again?

Roger came up with an idea.

'How about a boxing-glove?' The boys had brought along two pairs of boxing-gloves so that they might amuse themselves when life on board became too monotonous – if it ever did.

Roger slipped down to the cabin and brought back a glove. And a thimble!

Crab, standing by, was contemptuous.

'Do you think you're going to stop that brute with a boxing-glove and a thimble?'

The thimble was a big one, for a seaman's use. Hal caught the idea at once and gave his smart younger brother an admiring grin.

He put the solid steel thimble over the point of the sword,

then drew the boxing-glove on over the thimble. With his knife he cut notches in the sword and laced the glove to the notches so firmly that it could not come off.

Then water was pumped into the tank. The swordfish slowly revived. He swam lazily about. Then he backed and made a rush at the side of the tank. The boxing-glove harmlessly thumped the wall and bounced off.

Time and again the four-hundred-pound fish threw his weight into a swift plunge only to have the blow cushioned by that mysterious bulbous thing on the end of his sword. Finally he gave up making a battering ram of himself and turned his attention to the meal of fresh fish that had been poured into his tank.

'Land!' called Omo from the masthead.

Captain Ike peered ahead. 'It's land sure enough.'

Hal and Roger strained their eyes but could see nothing that looked like land.

But they did see something very strange. Straight ahead just over the horizon was a brilliant green cloud. Perhaps it wouldn't be right to call it a cloud – it was more like a light, a luminous glow.

One might see a greenish tint in the sky at sunrise or sunset, but whoever saw green in the middle of the morning?

It burned with a wavering light as if it were made of flame or gas or rippling water. It seemed to dissolve and flow away and then come back as strong as ever.

'What in the world is it?' Hal asked Omo who had now descended to the deck and seemed much amused by Hal's bewilderment.

'It's the Bikini atoll,' Omo replied. 'Not that we can see the atoll, but we know it is there by that glow in the sky.'

'What makes the glow?'

'Reflection from the lagoon. It has a floor of white sand and coral and is very shallow in some places – that makes the water appear a very light green – and it makes a mirage in the sky. You can see the mirage for half a day before you can see the island.'

Late in the afternoon Bikini reared its palms above the horizon. As the ship drew nearer Hal and Roger drank in the beauty of the first coral atoll they had ever seen.

It was like a necklace of pearls laid out on the sea. It was a great circle of coral reef surrounding a lagoon. The waves roared white on the reef, but the lagoon inside was calm and glowed with an aquamarine light. It was like a lake set down in the middle of the ocean. The captain said the lagoon was large, some twenty miles across.

Tiny coral polyps had industriously built up this long reef. Seeds of palms and plants that had drifted across the ocean had washed up on the reef and sprouted in the decaying coral and sand. The result was that here and there along the reef an island had formed, a green lovely island contrasting sharply with the barren whiteness of the rest of the reef.

Some of these islands were little fellows, only about as long as the *Lively Lady*. Some were a mile long. But they were all very narrow. In every case only a few hundred yards separated the ocean shore from the shore of the lagoon.

At three points the reef was broken and it was possible to sail through into the lagoon. The *Lively Lady* headed for the south-eastern passage. The ship was sailing full before a strong wind and yawed dangerously as the following seas threw her stern this way and that. The tide poured in through the entrance like water through a funnel and savage conflicting currents thrashed the ship and sought to throw her upon the sharp coral. But Captain Ike knew his schooner and brought her in safely upon the quiet green mirror of the ocean lake. He hove-to and dropped anchor a cable's length from the gleaming white beach of a palm-covered islet.

Hal studied the captain's chart. The map showed twenty islands on the coral reef. The one close at hand was named Enyu. Others bore such names as Bikini, Aomoen, Namu, Rukoji, Enirikku, and – a real jaw-breaker – Vokororyuru.

In the north-east corner of the lagoon was a cross.

'What does the cross mean?' asked Hal.

'That's where the atom bomb tests were held.'

'Aren't you afraid of radioactivity?'

'Not any more,' said the captain. 'Those explosions were set off in 1946. Of course they made everything radioactive – the soil, the coconuts, even the fish. But now scientists report the place safe for human beings – provided they don't stay too long.'

'What happened to the natives who were here before the test?'

'There were one hundred and sixty-five of them living here. They and their King Juda were moved to Rongerik Island. It's a hundred and thirty miles east.'

'Wasn't that pretty tough – being rooted out of their home islands?'

'Pretty tough,' Captain Ike admitted. 'They didn't like Rongerik. There were no fish there and few food plants. The king appealed to the U.S. Navy to save them from starvation. So they were moved again – to Ujelang Island.'

'And they're still there?'

'Still there. But not very happy about it. Their old way of life has been ripped to pieces. The island is poor compared with these. The people have to depend upon the American Navy for food. They've lost their interest in life.'

'Hard luck,' sympathized Hal. 'But I suppose there was nothing else that the navy could have done. The tests had to be made. Will there be any more tests here?'

'Hard to say. But now the main proving ground is Eniwetok atoll. It's about two hundred miles farther west. We'll pass it.'

'I suppose the natives were shipped out of there too?'

'One hundred and forty-seven of them.' The captain's leather face crinkled in a smile around his sharp blue eyes. 'Oh well,' he said, 'it don't pay to get too sentimental about these kanakas. They've always been pushed around and I guess they always will be.'

The dinghy was lowered and all went ashore. It was good to feel solid ground underfoot. The island was a lush and lovely garden. If the trees had been injured by the atomic bomb blast there was little sign of it left. Nature had triumphed in spite of the most devastating blow that man could strike.

It took only half an hour to walk around the island. It was uninhabited. As night came on the men sat around the small campfire and ate a picnic supper. Hal noticed that Omo had wandered away down the beach, perhaps to enjoy the stillness of the lagoon under the night sky. During these past days he had felt strangely drawn towards Omo. He admired his even disposition, his patience and cheerfulness, his skill in handling the schooner, and his quiet courage. He wondered what Omo was thinking now that he had come back to the sort of islands he loved.

He excused himself and wandered down the beach. He found Omo leaning against a coconut tree and looking out over the lagoon. Hal joined him. Omo seemed so wrapped up in his reverie that Hal did not speak.

Now the lagoon was black instead of green. It looked like a sheet of black glass. It reflected blue-white Vega, yellow Arcturus, fiery-red Antares. A thousand other pinpoints of light stabbed its surface. In a few hours it would reflect the Southern Cross, quite visible here although Bikini was a few degrees north of the equator.

There was no sound except the muffled roar of the surf on the outer edge of the reef. The islands across the lagoon were dark.

'I was here once long ago,' said Omo. 'People lived here then. It was a happy place. Now it is very sad.'

'But it had to be,' Hal replied. 'I mean, the atom bomb tests and all that.'

'I know, I know. I blame no one.'

They sat down on the bank that shelved to the beach.

'Omo,' said Hal, 'how does it come that you speak English so well? I thought everybody down here spoke pidgin-English or – what do you call it? – bêche-de-mer.'

Omo's white teeth gleamed in a smile. 'I am glad you like my English. I learned it from an American missionary lady. She was very good – she taught our people much. Some of our other visitors were not so kind.'

Hal did not need to ask what he meant. The early European and American visitors to these waters had been more interested in copra and pearls than in kindness. They had given the natives their diseases, debauched them with their strong liquors, and slaughtered them with firearms. And was this cruelty a thing of the past? He remembered what Crab had said the other day: 'Let him sink. He's only a kanaka anyhow.' Had Omo heard him say it?

'Omo,' Hal said, 'I want you to do me a favour.'

Omo turned towards him eagerly. 'Anything in the world!'

'I have heard that your people have a custom of exchanging names. Two friends swap names as a sign that they are blood brothers and are ready to give their lives for each other. Would you be willing to swap names with me, Omo?'

Omo tried to answer, but choked with emotion. Hal caught the glint of starlight on a tear rolling down the brown man's cheek. Then Omo's powerful hand grasped his.

'It shall be so,' said Omo. 'In the depths of our hearts you shall be Omo and I shall be Hal. What we would do for ourselves we will do for each other.'

7 | Argument with an octopus

ROGER could never seem to get over the idea that this trip was a lark arranged for his special amusement.

His chief object in life was to have a good time. His brother could be as serious as he liked. But as for him, he was going to have some fun.

So, instead of hunting specimens along the reef the next morning, he stripped to his shorts and dived in for a cool swim.

This was the ocean side of the reef. The ocean was quiet this morning except for a lazy swell.

Hal saw his brother dive into the sea and smiled tolerantly. The kid was too young to work for long at a time. Let him enjoy himself.

Hal followed Omo, Crab, and the captain as they walked along the reef, peering over the edge. He saw a baby octopus in the shallows, then another, and another. Each was about as big as a plate. Omo picked up several of them, saying that he would cook them for lunch. In the islands, octopus tentacles were considered quite a choice titbit.

Roger was a powerful swimmer for his age. He was quite at home either on the surface or under water. Now he chose to swim straight down a couple of fathoms, keeping his eyes open and enjoying the marvellous coral formations.

A hole appeared in the reef wall and he swam through it into a cave. Sunlight striking a shelf of coral was reflected into the cave and filled it with a soft blue light. It was a place of bewildering beauty. Here the coral polyps had shown their skill as architects and the floor and walls were covered with fairy castles and palaces in blue, white, rose, and green coral.

But Roger was getting winded and could not stay to enjoy the scene. He was about to swim out and up when he noticed that the water did not extend to the top of the cave.

He rose until his head emerged. There was just room for his head between the surface of the water and the cavern roof.

A mischievous idea crept into his mind. What a joke it would be if he stayed here just long enough to get the folks a little worried.

He knew they had seen him dive in. If he didn't come up they would think he had drowned. They would have to dive in and hunt for him and it wasn't likely that they would happen upon this cave.

Perhaps they'd appreciate him more if they thought for a little while that he was dead.

He turned on his back and floated. He could breathe easily. The coral reef above him was so porous that it admitted plenty of air.

He could vaguely hear shouts above him and the splashing of divers into the sea. He lay quietly, chuckling to himself.

At the end of about ten minutes he filled his lungs with air and swam down and out of the cave. He did not come straight up but swam under water some twenty yards along the shore to where he knew some palm trees grew close to the edge.

Then he rose softly, slipped out of the water without a splash, and hid behind a palm.

The first thing he heard was Hal's agonized voice saying, 'I don't know how I'll ever explain this to Father. I should have kept a closer eye on him.'

Then Captain Ike: 'Poor kid! Such a nice kid too. I'm all broken up, that's what I am,' and he ended with what sounded very much like a snuffle.

Even crusty Crab had something nice to say. Omo, panting from his last dive into the sea, fell back upon something the missionary lady had taught him. He tried to comfort Hal by reminding him that he would meet his brother in Heaven.

Roger could not keep down a snort of glee. Then he stepped out from behind the palm tree, roaring with laughter.

He was still laughing and crying all at once when the captain, Crab, and Omo held him down while Hal administered a whale of a spanking.

'That'll hold you for a while, you crazy spalpeen,' fumed his angry elder brother. He was left flat on the reef, sick with laughter, while his annoyed companions resumed their search for specimens.

'That'll teach you to hide behind trees,' Hal flung back.

Roger stood up. 'But you've got it all wrong,' he chuckled. 'I wasn't behind the tree – most of the time. Look. I'll prove it to you. Keep your eye on the tree.'

And he dived again.

But Hal had had enough of his brother's pranks. Why should he keep his eye on the tree? Roger wouldn't come up behind the same tree – it would be another this time.

The idea of a submarine retreat never occurred to him. He went on after the others down the beach.

As Roger swam into the cave he caught a glimpse of what looked like a huge snake stretched across the cave floor. One end of it disappeared into a black hole at the back of the cave.

When he had reached the surface and taken breath he looked down to study this strange creature more carefully. It was hard to see plainly because it took on the colour of its background. Where it lay on pink coral it was pink, and it was blue, white, or black, according to what lay behind it.

Presently Roger made out another like it, and then two

more. The ends of them all went up to the black hole.

And what was that at the hole? It was half in and half out, something almost as black as the hole. It was a bulbous baggy mass of no definite shape. In it were two eyes. They were small slanting eyes with a frightfully evil expression and they were looking straight at him.

A chill ran through him as he realized that here, lying doggo, waiting for a victim to come too close, concealing itself by taking on the colour of its surroundings like a chameleon, was a full-grown octopus!

He was horrified but not surprised. Where there were little fellows in the shallows it was only natural that there might be bigger ones in deeper water. But he hadn't expected to share the same cave with one.

Taking a deep breath – for he knew that it might have to last him a long time if he tangled with this beast – he swam down towards the entrance with strong swift strokes. His head, arms, shoulders emerged into the blessed freedom of the ocean. Another stroke and he would be safe.

Something lightly slipped around his ankle. He was gently drawn back into the cave. He struggled to free himself. But the grip on his ankle was as firm as it was gentle.

Roger's hand went to his knife – or where his knife should be. But the knife and the belt to which it was attached were with the slacks he had stripped off and left on the reef above.

He seized the tentacle and tried to pull it away from his ankle. He could see that the tentacle was lined with two rows of suction cups. He got his ankle loose from the beast's vacuum grip – only to feel another tentacle go around his other leg, and another slide softly over his shoulder.

Now he yelled for help. Hal and the rest must be on the reef just above his head waiting for him to come up. They would hear him and come.

The yell used up most of his precious breath. If he did

not get air in the next half-minute he would pass out. He fought to reach the top of the cave. Seizing the lumps of coral that projected from the wall he tried to pull himself up.

The Old Man of the Sea kept a heavy arm over his shoulder. Roger could not dislodge it. With all his might he thrust his shoulder forward, jamming the tentacle against some sharp coral.

A sound exactly like a human groan came from the octopus. It relaxed its grip on his shoulder and he was able to slide free. His legs were still held. But he managed to break water and draw breath.

Then he yelled – and how! He had never yelled as loud at any ball game.

'Hey, Hal! For the love o' Mike! Octopus! Hal! Hurry!'

He felt a sharp pang of remorse for the trick he had played upon his brother. Pretending he was in trouble, he had seriously worried his friends. Now that he was in real trouble – would they think he was just fooling again? The boy who had cried 'Wolf' once too often . . .

The octopus was tugging at his legs. He yelled again and put his heart into it.

'Hal! Honest! An octopus's got me!'

He just had time to gulp air before he was dragged again beneath the surface.

Now the great arms were closing in on him, around his shoulders, his chest, his stomach, his legs.

He remembered the boa-constrictor of his Amazon adventure. But these tentacles were like eight boa-constrictors all attacking at once. They began tightening upon him, cramping his stomach, crowding his lungs, retarding his heartbeat. A little more of this terrific pressure and his heart must stop.

The light was partly shut off as someone or something came into the entrance of the cave. It must be Hal. Roger twisted about so that he could see. What he saw was the great head of a tiger shark. The scavenger of the sea had smelled the blood running from Roger's scratches made by the coral.

The unexpected visit had a remarkable effect upon the octopus. It at once loosened its grip on the boy's body. It turned an angry purple.

Its sac of a body swelled as it drew in water. The sac suddenly contracted and the octopus shot like a torpedo towards its enemy. It went through the water so fast that the eye could hardly follow it.

It was very much like a jet plane or a rocket. The water suddenly expelled from the sac through a funnel propelled the beast forward at terrific speed, with the tentacles closed in and trailing behind. It was quite like a comet with a tail.

The eight mighty arms with their hundreds of suckers slapped around the impudent fish who had dared hope to steal the octopus's dinner. Just outside the entrance to the cave was fought a battle royal. Roger could get only an occasional glimpse of thrashing fins and tightening tentacles. The visibility was made worse when the octopus emitted a great black cloud from its ink sac.

It would be suicide to venture out just now. Roger breathed and rested and hoped against hope that the two contenders might move far enough away so that he could escape.

He shouted again – but he no longer had confidence that his friends were near by.

Now he could see nothing but the black cloud. The two mortal enemies might be whirling inside it, or they might be gone.

He must take a chance. He drew breath and went down. Half-way to the cave entrance he twisted and rose again to the roof – for he had seen the Old Man of the Sea peering into the cave from the ink cloud.

It was alone. Evidently it had triumphed over its rival.

Now it came in through the cave door, walking on its tentacles, pirouetting like a dancer or a gigantic spider.

It stepped along delicately, almost gracefully. It was like a cat stalking a mouse. Rainbow colours flitted over its body. Roger had learned in his talks with Captain Ike and Omo that this was a sign of great anger.

For the octopus was quite capable of emotions. It could be affectionate with its young and furious with enemies. It had a highly developed brain far finer than that of any fish, eyes that were similar to human eyes, and it was as cunning as a fox.

Roger could see the beast's mantle swelling. He yelled again, for he knew that the final struggle was now only a matter of seconds.

Then the mantle squeezed tight like the bulb of a squirt-gun. The octopus catapulted up through the water and whipped its arms around its dinner.

A boy with less fighting spirit than Roger would have given up now. He kept battling and, at the same time, trying to remember. What was it Omo had told him? A way the islanders sometimes used to conquer the terror of the deep. Something about a nerve centre between the eyes. If you could get at it, the beast could be paralysed.

He would win yet. He would not only beat this devil, he would take it alive. They wanted an octopus for the collection. Perhaps they would forgive the scare he had given them if he made good now.

He stayed with his head above the water as long as possible, clinging to the coral. Then the octopus with a terrific jerk pulled him under. But his lungs were full of air and his heart full of fight. Only he did not struggle this time against the enveloping arms. He saved his strength.

He was drawn closer to the two evil eyes. They were exactly like the small slanting eyes of an angry rhino such as the one he had seen maim a foreman at this father's animal farm.

The monster's jaws, until now concealed under the mantle, opened to receive him. They were shaped like the beak of a parrot, but many times as large. They could smash a coconut or a robber crab at one crunch – so what chance would his head have?

And yet he let himself be drawn closer.

He pretended to be weaker than he was. The Old Man of the Sea would think that he had given up. The octopus did not clutch him so tightly now – it did not need to. This was going to be an easy victim after all. The tentacles drew the morsel closer.

He felt as if his lungs would burst. But he must stick it out a little longer. Where was that thing? – Omo had said it was just between the eyes. All the nerves of the body met there in a little ganglia about the size of a pea.

Yes, there it was – a little bump, like a wart or a pimple. He nerved himself. He looked straight into the hating eyes and could not help dreading that they would read his mind. He tried to relax his muscles and hang limp so that his sudden move, when he made it, would be unexpected.

With a sharp twist he lunged at the pealike protuberance and caught it firmly between his teeth. Then he bit – hard.

The monster groaned like a human being in great agony. It struggled weakly and clouded the water with ink. The suckers lost their vacuum control and the tentacles fell away from the boy's body.

The first thing Roger did was to come up to breathe – and just in time. He rested for a few moments. The octopus hung, inert, below him.

He hoped he had bitten just hard enough to paralyse the beast. Omo had said that an octopus could be killed this way. When the creature did not move he began to worry.

He submerged now, gripped one tentacle of the octopus, and drew the limp giant out of the cave. Although it had a tremendous spread it was not heavy, having no bone structure except its beak.

When his head came out into the sunlight he breathed a
mighty sigh of thankfulness. The world had never looked so
good. Perhaps Roger was several years older now than he
had been half an hour before – older and wiser. He had a
better perspective upon life and death.

He crawled out of the water. He saw the others far down
the reef. He shouted and they turned to look. When they
saw what he lifted out of the water they came running back.

'For heaven's sake!' exclaimed Hal. 'What have you got
there? The Old Man of the Sea himself! Is he dead?'

'I hope not,' Roger said. 'How can we get him to the
ship?'

'Keep him in the water,' warned Omo. 'The sun will kill
him. I'll get the dinghy – it's on the other side of the island.'

While Omo went to bring the boat around, Roger re-
counted his adventure. Hal's face went pale and green by
turns. Crab's eyes looked as if they would pop out of his
ugly face.

'Well,' remarked Captain Ike when Roger had finished,
'you may have a bit o' mischief in you, but you've got some
guts too.'

Omo rowed up with the dinghy. 'Just sit in the stern and
tow him,' he advised Roger. 'Keep him under water.'

They rowed through the pass into the lagoon and to the
ship's side. A line was slipped around the pulpy mass and it
was drawn up and plopped into a tank without delay.

It was far too big for the tank if it chose to extend its
arms. Each of those boa-constrictor tentacles was twelve
feet long. 'But he doesn't need to stretch his arms,' Omo
said. 'He's used to living hunched up like a ball.'

The monster was beginning to show signs of life. A light
came into the eyes. Colours began to play across the body.
The tentacles began to squirm.

The mantle swelled. Then the creature shot like a rocket
across the tank, coming with a crash against the far wall. It
shot in the other direction and encountered another wall.

Finding itself a prisoner it began to dash about wildly using its four methods of locomotion – for the octopus can walk on its tentacles, slide along on its mouth, swim by waving its arms, or project itself by jet propulsion. It began to chew at its own arms.

'They do that,' said Captain Ike. 'Sometimes they eat their own arms off when they're caught. They're just so blamed mad they don't care what they do. Your man won't want an octopus with no arms.'

But Omo had already come, tugging the answer, an empty iron barrel. He lowered it into the tank. He laid it on its side, completely under water.

The octopus immediately rocketed into its dark interior and drew its tentacles in after it.

'On the sea bottom,' said Omo, 'they always like a black hole like that. He'll feel at home there.'

8 | Hurricane

SINCE dawn everyone on board had been irritable and nervy.

The *Lively Lady* had left Bikini and was once more sliding 'downhill' on her way to Ponape. The wind was fair, the sea was normal, and there was no apparent reason for uneasiness.

But the air was hot, the breeze was no longer refreshing. It seemed to come out of a steam bath. Or it was like the close, thick air in the bilge of a ship.

It had no life in it. It nauseated you – it made you feel as if you would like to be rid of your breakfast.

And the sky, instead of being blue, was a sort of white-black.

Now, nothing can be white and black at the same time, yet that was the way of it. A sort of pallid darkness was filling the firmament and pressing down upon the ship and upon the spirits of those aboard her. The hour was twelve noon but you would have supposed it to be early dawn or late twilight.

Hal stood near the binnacle, sextant in hand, trying to get a noon reading. Then with the *Nautical Almanac* he could compute the ship's position.

Hal had been studying navigation with a will. Not only was it a useful thing for anybody to know: it was especially important for him – if he was to carry out the secret instructions of Professor Richard Stuyvesant.

A dozen times a day the figures he had never written down drummed in his mind – North Latitude 11° 34′, East Longitude 158° 12′ – the position of Pearl Lagoon.

There was a puzzle he had not yet solved. How was he to reach the island without disclosing the secret of its position? If the captain and Crab and Omo went along, all three would learn the location of the pearl atoll.

He thought he could trust Omo. He was not so sure of the captain and Crab. Could they be in with the gang that had threatened the professor and ransacked his files? Some remarks they had dropped made him suspicious.

Anyhow, he would feel safer if they did not accompany him and Roger to Pearl Lagoon. But he could never reach the island without the help of someone who understood navigation.

The answer was plain – he must understand it himself. He must learn to steer a vessel by sun, stars, and chronometer so he could bring it to that pinpoint in the sea, North Latitude 11° 34′, East Longitude 158° 12′.

How he would get rid of the captain and Crab was a problem he had yet to figure out.

Captain Ike broke in on his thoughts.

'Having trouble?'

'Can't get the sun sharp,' complained Hal.

Captain Ike looked up. A whitish glow had taken the place of the usually clear-cut sun. In the increasing darkness, the sky looked like the face of a ghost.

Captain Ike looked at the barometer. It usually stood well above thirty. Now it had dropped close to twenty-nine.

'Looks like we're in for a blow,' said Captain Ike.

It seemed an odd statement to Hal because the wind, instead of getting stronger, was growing weaker. Now it came only in fitful puffs. The sails sagged and slatted. The booms swung idly. The wind had failed altogether.

'What's the matter with everything?' inquired Roger emerging from below where he had been resting from his bout with the octopus the day before. His body was covered with ring-shaped welts left by the beast's vacuum cups. 'I can't seem to breathe.'

It was as if a great blanket had been pressed down upon the ship and its occupants, smothering them under its folds.

'Hurricane!' declared Captain Ike. Never was there anything less like a hurricane than this breathless calm. 'Omo, make everything tight! Crab, sails down!' Crab stepped sluggishly towards the mainsail halyards. 'Step lively!' cried the captain. 'There's not a minute to lose.' He with Hal and Roger tackled the jib and staysails.

The halyard of the upper staysail jammed in the block.

'Got to get up there and free it,' panted the captain. He looked around for his crew. Omo and Crab were busy. He himself was a bit old and bulky to attempt the climb to the masthead. Roger was wobbly after yesterday's tussle.

Hal jumped to the ratlines and began to climb. Up past the lower crosstrees, past the crow's-nest, to the peak. He loosed the halyard and the staysail came rattling down.

Meanwhile things were happening on deck. Omo lashed down the hatches and the dinghy, braced the octopus's barrel with two-by-fours so that it would not roll, and saw to it that the lids of all tanks were made secure. Crab, who could be fast enough when he wished but took delight in being as slow as molasses when he was asked to be quick, reefed the mainsail and jib and took the staysail below. There he stopped in the storeroom to take a swig of his favourite liquor.

The captain started the engine. He began to bring the ship about to face whatever danger was coming. The thing to do was to heave-to with the ship's nose to the storm until it blew over.

The *Lively Lady* was lively with sails but took her time to respond to an engine. She was only half-way about when the thing came.

Hal at the masthead saw it coming. He could not get down before it would arrive. He managed to drop into the crow's-nest and there he crouched to meet it.

It was a wave that towered far above him, high though he was. A single gigantic wave with not a ripple to announce its coming and no billows to be seen in its train. Hal gazed up and into it. Its top was like an overhanging cliff. The green over-curl was edged with white foam. Untold tons of water hung between sea and sky ready to crash down upon the *Lively Lady*.

The ship, broadside on, began to climb the mountain. She listed to starboard until her masts were horizontal and Hal looked down from his perch not upon the deck but into the glassy sea.

Should he jump clear now? Nothing afloat could stand this. The schooner was bound to roll bottom-side up. Then he might be tangled in the rigging and never get to the surface.

But something made him trust the *Lively Lady* and hang on. He flinched as the overhang descended upon him. He was struck a crushing, stunning blow. He could never have hung on in the face of it but he did not need to, for he was so jammed against the mast and the rail of the crow's-nest that he could not escape if he wanted to.

The falling sea knocked the wind out of his body. He breathed stinging salt water into his lungs. He felt his strength going. And yet the whole thing seemed unreal. How could he be drowned forty feet above deck?

Where was Roger? Had he been washed overboard? So this was a hurricane! He had never thought it would be like this. Would they ever come out of this wave?

Then the water slipped away from him with a dragging pull on his body. The mast seemed to be upright once more. He looked down to where the deck should be. There was nothing but a swirling surge of sea.

Then it washed away and the deck leaped into view. His eyes searched for Roger. There he was. His smart kid brother had lashed himself to the foremast. He looked more dead than alive, but he was still with the ship. The captain had flattened himself out on the floor of the cockpit. Omo had come through the deluge like a seal and was already busy trying to repair a damaged rudder.

Crab was nowhere to be seen.

Crab had never known a drink to take effect so fast. He had no sooner swallowed it than he was struck a terrific crack on the skull, hurled against the bulkhead, pelted with boxes, bales, crates, and cans and covered with flour from a burst bag. Half-buried by supplies, he lay on the wall, with his head on the ceiling. Then there was a roll and the ship's stores left him, only to come flying back the next instant, pummelling him black and blue.

He struggled through the welter of flying things to the door which had slammed shut. He could not open it. It was not locked. It was never locked. Yet with all his strength he couldn't budge it. There was a terrific roaring outside.

For the wind had come at last. It had sealed the door as securely as if it had been nailed. The room again lay on its side. Crab stood on the wall and battled with the door.

But things had stopped flying about. He was a fool to try to get out, Crab thought. He could rest here and let the others work. After all, they couldn't blame him for it wasn't his fault that the door was jammed. He stretched himself out on the wall.

During the interval between the great wave and the wind Hal had slipped to the deck. The ship lying broadside to the wind was on her beam ends. Her deck was steeper than the roof of a house. She did not roll. She seemed held there by a mighty hand. The water had been as smooth after the wave as before it, but it was beginning to kick up now under the gale.

The plucky little engine laboured to bring her about. As it gradually succeeded the deck levelled out. The great wave rolled away to leeward like a moving skyscraper.

As the ship put her nose into the storm those on deck got the full force of the wind. It moved in on you like a solid wall. When Hal tried to face it it blew his eyes shut and crowded into his lungs until he thought he would burst with the pressure. He would have been swept away like a leaf if he had not taken the precaution of lashing himself to the mast. Now he squirmed around to get on the lee side of it.

He could believe the captain when he told him later that the force of the hurricane was twelve on the Beaufort scale. This was twice the force of the average strong gale which rarely registered above six.

A strange elation tingled through his veins. He had always wondered what a hurricane was like. Of course he had read about it – how it got its name from the devil Hurakan, the thunder-and-lightning god of the Indians of Central America; how the same thing was called a typhoon in the western Pacific after the Chinese word *taifung*, meaning great wind; how it went elsewhere by such names as chubasco, ciclon, huracan, torbellino, tormenta, tropical. But whatever you chose to call it, it was something to remember for a lifetime.

Behind the mast it was as hard to get air as it had been to avoid getting too much before the mast. The wind slid by in two currents, one on each side, with such speed that between them a vacuum was created. Water splashed up on the forecastle was at once atomized and blown aft as spray.

It was dangerous spray as Hal found when he experimentally put out his hand. The hand was flung back at him with terrific force. The fingers were bleeding where they had been stabbed by the shafts of spray. The arm felt as numb as if a bolt of electricity had gone through it. Hal estimated that the wind must be travelling at a good hundred and fifty miles an hour.

It did not take such a wind long to end the momentary calm after the passing of the big wave. The sea came alive with leaping hills of water. The ship, which had been on an even keel for a few moments, began to pitch wildly. It climbed the slopes with its nose in the air and plunged head first into the troughs.

Hal was glad of the mast and the lashings that held him

to it. Roger was lashed to the other mast. Omo continued to skip about the dipping deck like a monkey, but Captain Ike lay wedged in the cockpit. His hand gripped the lower spokes of the wheel. There was still no sign of Crab. He ought to be on deck helping his crew-mate battle with flying gear and rigging.

In the meantime, all was not well with Crab. His dream of a quiet siesta while the storm raged was not working out. He had a few moments of peace to gloat over the jammed door that locked him away from his labours.

Then the sudden pitching of the ship in the wind-whipped sea began to play football with him. He was flung from the floor to the wall and from the wall to the floor. There was a bunk at one side of the room and he got into it. It threw him out. He got in again and was again tossed out amid a shower of cans. Everything loose seemed to come alive and to take delight in pelting him. It was like being inside the crazy house in an amusement park.

In a frenzy of fear he attacked the door. It was as solid as a bulkhead. He backed off and ran, crashing it with his shoulder. Nothing happened except to his shoulder.

He tried to shield his head from the flying missiles. He beat upon the door with his fists and yelled blue murder – well knowing he could not be heard. He flung a heavy box against the door. But on the other side was the heavier hand of the wind. He was a prisoner in a torture chamber.

He began to repent of his sins. If he got out of this place alive he would never drink again, he would never try to get out of work, he would be a model of sweetness and light.

As if an angel had been waiting for just such resolutions the door against which he was leaning suddenly opened in a lull of the wind and he fell head over heels into the corridor. The door slammed shut again, leaving him in peace.

He promptly forgot his fine promises, braced himself between the bulkheads in a curled-up position and took a nap.

The wind had grown fitful. It came in gusts and gasps, then stopped altogether. The roar had been so great that Hal was deafened by the silence. The clouds of flying spray disappeared and the blue sky broke out.

'We're through it!' shouted Roger.

Hal was not so sure.

'That's only half of it,' growled Captain Ike.

The wind of a hurricane goes around in a circle. It may move at a rate of anywhere from a hundred to two hundred miles an hour. But the entire revolving mass does not move forward much faster than twelve miles an hour.

At the centre of this merry-go-round is the 'eye' of the hurricane, a quiet spot with little or no wind.

'We're in the centre,' Captain Ike said. 'Half an hour perhaps – then we'll catch it on the other side.'

Hal and Roger unlashed themselves to go to Omo's assistance. The canvas had torn out of the gaskets. The running gear was a tangle of lines knotted by the wind. The dinghy was about to pull away.

The men gasped as they worked. The air was suffocatingly thin and hot.

It was hard to understand at first why the ship should roll and pitch worse than ever. The waves were much higher than in the path of the wind. Here they had no pressure of wind to keep them under control. They shot up in great spouts fifty, sixty feet high. It seemed as if mines or torpedoes must be exploding under the surface to send up such geysers.

Huge pointed lumps of water as big as houses raced about madly in all directions, crashed into each other, sent up fountains of spray, fell away in a hundred waterfalls.

The confusion was due to the fact that from every point of the compass winds were blowing in towards this centre of calm. And so the waves popped up helter-skelter and went wildly north, south, east, west, anywhere. It was anarchy, it was chaos.

But the *Lively Lady* took it. In such a sea a passenger ship or cargo steamer would have gone to Davy Jones's locker. But a small craft can often weather such treatment better than a large one.

One reason is that the wooden schooner is more buoyant than the steel steamship and rides the waves. Also a small craft can slide down one wave and climb another while the big ship lies across several waves and is attacked by all of them; and the parts of her hull that are not supported may buckle under the strain. The big ship resists the waves, the small craft goes with them.

So the *Lively Lady* shot heaven high and dropped into dark depths and flung herself this way and that so that it was hard to hang on – but she stayed on top.

Birds by the hundreds swept into the centre by the storm collected in the rigging. Noddies, boobies, and gulls slid about the deck and two big frigate birds settled in the dinghy. Thousands upon thousands of butterflies, moths, flies, bees, hornets, grasshoppers, were clustered on the masts and ratlines or buzzed about the faces of the men at work.

The ship had been headed north-east to keep her nose in the wind. Now the captain brought her around to south-west.

'What's that for?' Hal asked.

'When the wind comes again it'll be from the opposite quarter.'

And then it came – with a bang. Its arrival was so abrupt that Roger and Hal were all but swept overboard. The roar of the wind struck like a clap of thunder. The stinging spray began to cut into faces and hands. The blue sky was gone and there was nothing but that ghostly darkness streaming past.

The waves were lower, not much higher than the masts now, but they were all going one way and seemed to have a deadly purpose.

It was soon plain that the hurricane's second act was going to be worse than the first. Both wind and wave were more violent than before. Birds and insects disappeared as if by magic. Rigging was being blown to bits. The sails escaped from their lashings and went up into the wind in rags and tatters. The boom broke loose and swung murderously back and forth across the deck.

There was too much to do for Hal and Roger to consider the luxury of lashing themselves to the masts. They helped Omo – and wondered about Crab.

The ship was wrenched as if by giant hands. There was a rending sound aft and the wheel went lifeless.

'The rudder!' cried Captain Ike. 'It's gone!'

The ship's nose dropped away from the wind. She broached to and lay in the trough, rolling with a sickening wallow.

At every roll she took on tons of water that surged across the deck shoulder-deep and thundered down the companionway into the hold.

The captain already had the pumps working to clear the hold but water was coming on board too fast.

Crab's siesta came to a choking end. He woke to find himself under water, salt sea crowding down into his lungs. He got into action with remarkable speed, and struggled up to the deck, gasping and sputtering.

Nature evidently liked to play tricks with Crab. He had no sooner come on deck than a wave caught him and washed him over the rail.

'Man overboard!' shouted the captain.

The words were just out of his mouth when the backwash of the same wave that had carried Crab overboard carried him back and deposited him with a thump on the deck. The boys laughed to see the look of dumb surprise on his face.

'Get a grip on yourself,' said the captain sharply, 'or you'll be going over again.'

But no one had time to pay much attention to Crab. The Wind that Kills, as the Polynesians call the hurricane, seemed determined to do away with the *Lively Lady*.

The ship lurched violently, there was a tearing, splitting sound, and the mainmast fell. Still bound to the ship by stays, ratlines, and halyards, it dragged in the sea, listing the deck heavily to port. A few moments later the foremast went down, smashing the dinghy as it fell.

This was no longer an adventure. It was a tragedy. The *Lively Lady* was no longer a ship, she was a wreck. And the lives of those on board could not have been insured for tuppence.

'Rig a sea anchor!' bawled the captain.

With the hold full of water, every wave now rolled clear over the ship. To add to the torment, rain began to fall, not in drops but in bucketsful. Unbelievable weights of water dropped like sledgehammers on the heads and shoulders of the seamen.

Hal could now believe what he had been told of hurricane rain. In a certain Philippine hurricane more rain fell in four days than the average rainfall for a whole year in the United States.

It was almost more comfortable under a wave than under the flailing of the rain.

But there was no moment for rest – if a sea anchor were not rigged quickly the ship was going to founder with all hands.

The boys swung the fallen foremast parallel with the mainmast. They lashed the two together. They made fast a stout cable to the masts and looped the other end over mooring bitts on the bow of the vessel.

Then they cut the stays and lines that held the masts to the ship. The masts slid off the deck into the sea.

Since the ship was carried along by the wind, while the masts, half-submerged, were not, the effect of the sea anchor was to bring the bow of the ship up into the wind, so it met the waves head-on and the danger of foundering was a little diminished.

Another hour the gallant little ship struggled to stay above the surface.

Then, as suddenly as it had come, the wind howled away. Men who had been braced against the wind found themselves unbalanced for lack of it. They had become used to lying on it as a firm bed.

The blue sky appeared again. The sun blazed. The whirling wrack of the storm full of howling devils, and looking like a monstrous evil genie, bore off to the westward at about twelve knots.

For a time the sea, without the wind to hold it down, was worse than ever. Then it moderated and waves ceased to surge over the deck and pour into the hold. The pumps began to win. The ship rose.

Five exhausted men breathed a silent prayer of thanks.

Hal anxiously inspected the tanks. None of the lids had been dislodged and since he was always careful to keep the tanks full to the brim there had been no sloshing to injure the specimens. They seemed to have come through the experience better than their human friends.

'Do we abandon the masts?' Hal asked the captain.

'No. We'll tow 'em to Ponape. We can get them restepped there.'

And so, with a roughly repaired rudder, her proud sails replaced by a chugging engine, her masts dragging behind her, the unlively lady limped on to Ponape.

9 | Into the lost world

Now they were in little-known seas. Even Captain Ike
Flint had never been here before. They saw no ships, for
the regular ship lanes lie far to the north and south.

Between the two world wars this part of the Pacific had
been governed by the Japanese. They had jealously barred
all ships but their own from its waters. Its 2,500 islands had
no contact with the outside world except through Japan.
Non-Japanese travellers visited them at risk of their lives.

And it was still a shut-away world in spite of the fact that
it had been taken from Japan in World War II and was
now governed by the United States as a trust under the
United Nations.

Boys of the U.S. Navy stationed here felt as if they had
been marooned on the moon. So it was with some excite-

ment that they saw a strange craft enter the harbour of Ponape. They were going to have visitors!

Their excitement was shared by the visitors who were eager to step from the deck of the limping lady to the shores of the loveliest island they had yet seen.

'Isn't it a beauty!' exclaimed Hal, looking at the white reef, the blue lagoon inside it, and, inside that, the towering green skyscraper of an island. Its wildly picturesque mountains were dressed with groves of coconut palms, spreading mango trees, giant banyans, and hundreds of unknown varieties bearing brilliant flowers or heavy fruit. The old Spaniards were right – they had called this 'the garden island'.

And, unlike the low coral atolls, it evidently got plenty of rain. The high peaks invited storms. Even now around lofty Totolom peak there roared a black thunderstorm pierced with yellow shafts of lightning.

'Gosh!' said Roger, his eyes popping. 'They talk about Tahiti and Samoa and all that. Are they really any better than this?'

'Not near as fine,' declared Captain Ike, who had seen them.

'Then why do we never hear about this – gee, I don't even know how to pronounce it . . .'

'Po-nah-PAY is the way they say it. You don't hear about it because mighty few people have ever been here.'

'Look at Gibraltar!' cried Roger.

It did look like Gibraltar. But according to the chart it was the Rock of Chokach. It loomed 900 feet high over the harbour, its basaltic cliffs falling away so steeply as to defy climbers.

Through a gap in the reef the dismasted schooner putputted her way into the harbour. The lagoon was sprinkled with fairy islands. Between two of them, charming Takatik and Langar, Captain Ike dropped anchor in ten fathoms. The chart indicated dangerous shallows near shore.

There were no craft in the harbour except fishing boats and a few naval A.K.s and L.S.T.s. There was one plane to be seen – a tired-looking Catalina.

From the town of Ponape which nestled on a point of the mainland a launch put out. It came alongside and a smart young naval officer climbed on board. He made himself known as Commander Tom Brady, Deputy Military Governor of Ponape.

'You evidently got a taste of the hurricane,' he said.

'More than a taste,' admitted Captain Ike. 'Did you feel it here?'

'Luckily it slid by to the north of us. But one of our supply ships was in its path.'

'What happened?'

'It went down – all five thousand tons of it. It's a miracle that this little eggshell came through on top.'

Captain Ike proudly surveyed his battered schooner. 'Pretty stout little ship! Is there a place here where we can get her repaired?'

'Right around in the shipyard.'

'You'll want to see her papers,' said Captain Ike, producing them. 'And how about port charges?'

Commander Tom Brady laughed. 'Don't worry about that. We don't have enough visitors to have to levy port charges. You're the first, outside of Navy, in six months. How long do you stay?'

'That's for Mr Hunt to say. He's the master of this expedition.'

'Not long,' Hal said. 'While the captain is having the ship repaired I'd like to hire a motor-boat and make a little side trip – out to some of the small islands.'

There was a moment's silence. Brady seemed to be waiting for more details. But Hal had no intention of disclosing the nature of his errand to Pearl Lagoon, especially in the presence of witnesses.

'Fine,' said Brady, accepting the situation. 'We'll get you

a boat. But just now I know you'd all like to get ashore.
Pile into the launch.'

The captain, Roger, and Omo boarded the launch. Hal
was about to follow them when the captain said, 'Where's
Crab?'

'I'll find him,' said Hal, and went forward. Crab was not
in the forecastle. Hal returned aft and went down to look
in the storeroom. Crab was not there. A rustling attracted
his attention and he opened the door to his and Roger's
cabin.

There was Crab, rummaging through Hal's notebooks
and papers.

'What are you doing here?' Hal asked sharply.

'Nothing. Nothing at all,' Crab sullenly answered, and
pushed past Hal out of the door and up the companionway.
Hal followed him and they both dropped aboard the launch
without another word.

But Hal was thinking hard. Crab must have been looking
for information about the pearl island. Evidently he was in
with the plotters who had searched Professor Stuyvesant's
papers and threatened his life. They had put him aboard
the *Lively Lady* to get the information that they had failed
to get.

There was no use making a scene over it. But Hal knew
that whoever went with him to Pearl Lagoon, it would not
be Crab, and when the *Lively Lady* sailed again Crab
would not be a member of the crew.

The town of Ponape consisted mainly of Japanese stores
and houses built by the Japanese during the thirty years
they had held the island. In the outskirts were the thatch
homes of native brown Ponapeans.

Brady led the way to a Japanese house on the edge of a
bluff with a magnificent view across the harbour to the
towering Rock of Chokach.

'This is yours for as long as you want it,' he said. 'Make
yourselves at home.'

It was pleasant to lie at full length on the clean golden-yellow mats and look out over the blue lagoon dotted with green islets and the white sails of fishing boats, to the big rock backed by mountains thousands of feet high from whose cliffs tumbled silvery waterfalls.

'It's a sort of paradise,' said Hal.

But a worm of anxiety crept into his pleasure when he noticed that his party was one man short. Crab had again disappeared. What was that rascal up to now?

10 | The pearl trader

THERE was only one business street in the town and Crab had no difficulty in finding the Post Exchange.

He went in and looked about as if he had an appointment to meet someone here. A big man with a slight hunch in his back came towards him.

He did not smile or offer to shake hands. He only said gruffly:

'What took you so long? I saw your ship come in and I've been waiting here for half an hour.' He cast a suspicious glance at the clerk. 'Let's get out of here – go some place where we can talk.'

They went out into the street and turned at the next corner into a quiet lane. It wound away towards the hills between thatch huts set in lush gardens from which came the perfume of jasmine, frangipani, cinnamon, and aloes. Crab and his companion walked under a huge breadfruit tree from which hung fruits almost as big as footballs. They passed dozens of strange plants and trees – it was like going through a botanical garden.

The people were as fine as the trees. The men were more than six feet tall and powerful muscles rippled under their brown skins. Women wore white flowers in their hair. The babies were fat and cheerful. One of them sat in the road directly in the path of the big man. It laughed up at him.

He scooped it up with his foot and gave it a fling into the bushes, whereupon it broke into a loud wail.

Crab grew more and more nervous. It was evident that the man was in a bad temper. What Crab had to tell him would not make him any happier.

They came to a European-style house in a garden of orange and lemon trees, mangosteens, pomegranates, and peacock palms.

The man flung open the door and took Crab into a musty parlour. Two Ponapean servants promptly appeared – a woman who arranged the chairs and a man who asked in broken English whether master would like to have drinks.

'Get out of here!' roared the big man. 'Get out, both of you!' He helped them with a push or two and slammed the door after them.

'Dirty scum!' he said savagely. 'Curse their brown hides. If I was Uncle Sam I'd wipe 'em all clean off the island.'

He motioned Crab to sit down and took a chair facing him. He drew it close and leaned forward until his eyes were not two feet from Crab's. His hunched back gave him the appearance of a crouching lion about to spring.

'All right, out with it!' he snapped. 'Did you get the bearings?'

Crab could hardly breathe. He must stall for time. 'It was a hard job you gave me. I did my best. I listened in on him and his kid brother too but they never said anything. I went through all their things . . .'

'Never mind all that. Did you get the location of the island?'

'Can't say that I did but . . .'

He got no farther. A crashing blow from the big man's fist spun his head backwards, overturned his chair, and left him in a half-conscious heap on the floor. He got up shakily, dabbing at his bleeding nose.

'You'll be sorry for that, Kaggs.'

'You threaten me?' said the man called Kaggs, looming over Crab like a cliff about to fall upon his head. Looking down, Crab saw that the big man's hand held a revolver. He dropped back.

'I didn't mean anything, Mr Kaggs.'

For which he got a clout on the head with the butt of the

gun. 'Shut up! Don't use my name. I don't intend anybody to know me here.'

'Not know you? Why everybody knows you're the biggest pearl trader from Thursday Island to the Sulu Sea.'

'Down there they know. Not up here. Nobody thinks pearls up here. And these navy kids – what do they know about the Pacific? Most of them are just fresh out of school.'

'So if you aren't Merlin Kaggs – the crookedest pearl trader south of the equator – just who are you?'

The big man straightened slightly and nearly allowed a smile to take over his face. 'I am, if you please, the Reverend Archibald Jones. I am a missionary of the Go-Ye-Forth Church of America. I have flown here from San Francisco bearing glad tidings to the heathen of these benighted islands.'

Crab snorted. 'How can you make anybody believe you're a missionary? You, with two murders and a spell in San Quentin to your credit!'

'You'd be surprised, my friend. Even the devil can quote Scripture to his purpose. You see, my old man was a clergyman. I went to Sunday-school until it came out of my ears. I can quote the Bible like nobody's business. Perhaps my quotes aren't always letter perfect, but who's going to know that? My folks even started to make a preacher out of me. And don't you believe I wouldn't have made a good one. In prison I supplied the pulpit when the Reverend wasn't able to make it. I did pretty well too. No complaints from the parishioners.'

'But why the masquerade?' Crab inquired.

Kaggs' good humour disappeared. 'You ought to know,' he growled. 'I suspected you'd flop on this job. So I had to be ready to take over.'

'You mean you're going to play up to Hunt?'

'Sure. He's a good, God-fearing young man. He'll appreciate a gentleman of my qualities. I'll find a way to

get what I want out of him. Don't forget that I know a lot
already. I had the place wired. I heard every word he and
Stuyvesant said to each other. Only trouble is, they were
mum about the bearings. Then I followed his visitors when
they went away. Out into the country, to the Hunt Animal
Farm. That's how I learned their name was Hunt. From
there on it was easy – just a job of follow-up. And if you'd
done your part of it right we'd be in the clover now.'

He slipped his revolver back into the shoulder holster
under his coat and motioned Crab towards the door. 'You
can get along now. I've no more time to waste on you.'

But Crab did not move. 'Aren't you forgetting something?'

'Forgetting what?'

'To pay me.'

Kaggs bristled. 'Pay you – for what? You made a botch
of it. For all I know you got Hunt suspicious. I ought to
charge you – not pay you. Now get out of here before I
break you in two.' He made a lunge at Crab.

'I'll go,' whined Crab, making for the door. Only when he
had opened it and stood half-way out of it did he feel safe
to say, 'You'll be sorry. Don't forget I can spoil your little
game. I'm going to see Hunt right now.'

Kaggs' face darkened as his hand moved instinctively
towards his gun. But it stopped half-way. Kaggs was thinking fast. Crab was right – he could spill the beans. Kaggs
must stop him, but how? A killing in broad daylight
wouldn't do. A hundred people would hear the shot. Even
if he paid Crab something he couldn't be sure that the
sneak would keep his mouth shut. No, there must be a
better way.

His crafty face took on a look that was almost genial.
'Come to think of it,' he said, 'guess I've been a little too
hard on you. After all, you did your best. No man can do
more. Okay, I'll play ball with you. And I'm going to start
right now by treating you to drinks. Come with me.'

Crab regarded this sudden change of heart with suspicion, but the appeal of flowing liquor was too much for him.

He accompanied Kaggs. They returned to the main street, then branched off towards the bluff. Crab grew apprehensive for they seemed to be going straight towards the house occupied by the Hunt party.

But across the road from the house was a small liquor shop, and here Kaggs turned in.

He pushed through a group of Ponapean men resting under the trees after their early morning fishing and entered the door of the shop. A seedy-looking white man was behind the counter.

'Tony,' said Kaggs, 'here's a good friend of mine. Just arrived. I want to treat him to a drink. A lot of drinks.'

'Always glad to serve,' said Tony. 'I know how you feel. Must be nice to have a visitor in this God-forsaken place.'

'Makes me want to celebrate,' said Kaggs, glancing out of the window. 'I'd like my friend to have a real party. Crab, invite those fellows in. We'll set 'em up for everybody.'

'You can't do that,' said Tony hastily. 'It's against the law to likker up the brown people.'

'The law!' scoffed Kaggs. He produced a wad of paper money and waved it in Tony's face. 'Here's the law. Invite 'em in, Crab.'

Crab had no interest in entertaining Ponapeans, but if Kaggs wanted to pay for it, why not? He stepped out of the door and motioned to the men. He raised an imaginary glass to his lips. The fishermen were not slow in crowding into the shop.

Liquor is like dynamite to a Ponapean. Even without it he is one of the most warlike of Pacific islanders. With it, he goes wild. Because of this fact the sale or gift of liquor to natives was strictly forbidden.

'There's only one way I can do this,' said Tony to Kaggs. 'I can sell the liquor to you – and you'll have to take the responsibility for giving it to the Ponapeans.'

'Sure,' said Kaggs heartily. 'Say twenty dollars' worth of your hottest stuff. Here, Crab, it's your party,' and he pressed a twenty-dollar bill into the seaman's hand. Crab passed it over to Tony.

'Okay,' said Tony. 'Now if you'll just sign this receipt.'

'For what?' grumbled Crab.

'For the liquor – just to show I sold it to you. That puts me in the clear.'

Crab, anxious to get on with the real business of drinking, signed the receipt. He looked around for Kaggs, but the gentleman had disappeared.

Two hours later Hal and Roger were distracted from their contemplation of the beauties of nature by wild shouts on the other side of the house.

Captain Ike had gone back to the ship. Omo was in the kitchen exercising his skill as a cook.

'Omo,' called Hal. 'Go out and see what's doing.'

Omo went out. He came back in a moment to announce breathlessly, 'A riot. Crab He's been arrested.'

Hal and Roger tumbled out into the road. A dozen drunken Ponapeans milled about. Two were bleeding from knife wounds. Far down the road they saw Crab reeling in the firm grip of two naval police.

At one side of the road stood a tall man with a slight hunch in his back. He held a black book in his hand.

He strolled over to join Hal. 'Very unfortunate incident,' he said. 'Very unfortunate.' His pitying gaze embraced the group of befuddled Ponapeans.

'What happened?' asked Hal.

'That seaman plied them with liquor. A violation of the laws of God and man. Only another of the many afflictions that have been visited upon the innocent folk of these lovely islands!'

Hal looked after the retreating form of Crab. 'Who

notified the police?' he asked.

'I did,' said the stranger. 'I considered it my duty as a citizen and as a missionary.'

Hal noticed that the small black book in the man's hand was a Bible. How fortunate that the Ponapeans had a man of this sort to defend their interests.

'What will he get for it?' he asked.

'Too little,' sighed the missionary. 'Perhaps sixty days in jail – then possibly deportation to the States.'

Hal's impulse was to go to Crab's aid. Then he reflected that nothing better than this could possibly have happened. Crab was his enemy. He was in the plot against him and Professor Stuyvesant. So long as he was on the loose he was dangerous. In jail he could do no more harm. This was a stroke of luck.

'I hope it's a good jail,' he said.

'None better. He'll get a good bed and good food. It's more than he deserves.'

Hal extended his hand. 'I'm Hal Hunt. We just got in today on the *Lively Lady*. Pretty badly banged up by the hurricane.'

'Indeed!' said the stranger sympathetically as he took Hal's hand. 'My name is Jones. Reverend Archibald Jones.'

'You have a church in Ponape?'

'No – I too have just recently arrived. My ministry will not be in this island. There are already ministers and churches here. I feel that my call is to the small outer islands where the people have never had the opportunity to hear the Word. I am just now trying to arrange for transportation.'

'You expect to charter a boat?'

'Not exactly. My society would not wish to incur that expense. My hope is to find someone else who is making such a trip and go along as a passenger.'

'Which direction do you want to go?'

'North, south, east, west, it makes no difference. Where

ever there are islands, there are people who need our
message. But enough about me. Tell me of yourself – will
you be staying in Ponape?'

'No,' said Hal. 'I'm planning a trip too,' and felt like a
heel because he did not go on at once to invite this kindly
missionary to be his passenger. Caution held his tongue.

The Reverend Mr Jones did not press the matter. In fact
Hal thought he showed rare delicacy. He said, 'I hope you
will have a pleasant visit in Ponape, and a good trip. And
now I must go. I am expected at the sick-bed of one of my
native friends.' He shook hands again and was off.

A pretty good fellow, thought Hal. Decent of him not to
try to worm his way into my party when he learned we
were going to the islands. Evidently a man of some education. And he talked just like a missionary, thought Hal,
who had rarely heard a missionary talk. What a big, powerful fellow – but I suppose a missionary has to be pretty
strong to stand that sort of life. And pretty smart too. This
fellow looked smart – almost shrewd. Well, I suppose a
missionary has to be shrewd to get the natives to do
what is good for them. I've heard that a missionary down
here has to be able to do almost anything – build a
house, plant a farm, give people business advice, repair a
motor, heal the sick. This man seemed equal to all that and
more. He looks as if it would take a lot to stop him. I wish I
could help him. But I can't – at least not until I know more
about him.

And Kaggs' mind also was busy as he trudged off to the
supposed bedside of his supposed sick friend: He's a fine
young man. But the finer they are the harder they fall. I can
twist him around my finger like a string. And Crab – ha!
ha! – what a fool! I've put him where he can't make
any trouble. Now I'll let nature take its course. In a few
days this good-hearted young fellow is going to invite me to
take a trip with him to the islands.

His mind ranged far ahead. He would learn the location

of the pearl island by going there. Then he would somehow get Hal and his brother out of the way. Something would happen to them. He would fix it so that it would look like an accident. No one would ever be able to pin anything on him. He'd go back to the island with a pearling lugger, clean out the bed, dispose of the shell locally and take the pearls to New York and London. Every year he made it a practice to visit both cities to sell the pearls he had bought in the South Seas. He knew all the important jewellers. Nothing happened in the pearling industry, either in the South Seas or in the cities, that he did not learn about. He had known of Stuyvesant's project very early – when he had been in Celebes and the ship bearing the professor's Persian Gulf specimens had stopped there for supplies on its way to Ponape. He needed only one detail more – the position of the island.

Now he settled down comfortably to wait for Hal Hunt to present him with this information. Surely the young man would not refuse a helping hand to a poor faithful old missionary!

11 | The mysterious passenger

'WE have a boat for you,' announced Commander Tom Brady, calling upon the Hunts the next morning. With him he brought two smartly uniformed young men whom he introduced as Lieutenants Rose and Connor. 'It's not a very big boat – a thirty-footer.'

'That's big enough,' Hal said. 'How about the motor?'

'A good Hakata motor – made in Japan. You see, the boat is one of a fleet the Japs brought down for bonito fishing. Now it belongs to a native fishing guild – they'll let you use it for a modest fee.'

'What accommodation?'

'A cabin with four bunks. A galley. And a fishy smell.'

'It's a deal,' grinned Hal.

'I suppose,' said Brady to Captain Ike, 'you'll be going along as navigator.'

'No. I'll stay here to put the *Lively Lady* in shape. Hal will do his own navigating.'

Brady looked at Hal with new admiration. 'Explorer – scientist – and now navigator. You're doing pretty well for a young fellow.'

Hal reddened. Praise embarrassed him. And he didn't quite like being referred to as a young fellow. What if he was a bit younger than Brady, he was bigger and stronger and learning as fast as he could. 'I'm afraid I'm still pretty green on navigation,' he admitted. 'But perhaps I have enough of it for a short trip.'

'I'm sure you have,' said Brady cordially. 'It's too bad our police have had to deprive you of one of your crew.'

Hal understood that he was speaking of Crab. 'I wouldn't have taken him anyhow,' he said.

'And he'd be no use to me,' said Captain Ike vigorously.

'I don't know why I ever took him on in San Francisco. He came highly recommended. But was as lazy as a sea slug, as sour as a crab-apple, and always making trouble.'

'Well then,' said Brady, 'he ran true to form when he likkered up our natives. Our regulations are very strict on that point. So when the missionary notified us ...'

Hal saw a chance to learn more about the mysterious missionary.

'How about this Mr Jones?' he asked. 'Do you have any information on him?'

'I'm afraid we haven't,' Brady said. 'He flew here from San Francisco a week ago. He represents some mission organization in California. He seems to know other parts of the South Seas very well. I believe he's hoping to get a ride out to some of the islands. Apparently he's quite devoted to the welfare of the natives.'

'What he did yesterday proves that,' granted Captain Ike.

'Ponape isn't tough enough for him,' said Rose admiringly. 'He wants to go out and help the natives on some little island where life is really rugged. I'd say he's okay.'

'We need more like him,' added Connor.

Hal reflected that if he had been fooled by the Reverend Archibald Jones, he was not the only one. The man was either extraordinarily clever – so clever that he could bluff these four very able and intelligent men – or else he was on the level. Hal was ashamed that he had had any doubts of the missionary's integrity. He was ashamed too that he had not generously offered to take him as a passenger.

Brady was saying, 'You see how Rose and Connor feel about anyone who lends a hand to the natives. These two men may look to you like plain Navy – but Rose is a schoolteacher and Connor is a doctor. They're trying to see to it that the new generation of Ponapeans will grow up wise and healthy.'

'They eat it up,' Rose said. 'Education, I mean. You never saw kids so anxious to learn.'

'Is there much sickness?' Hal asked Dr Connor.

'A lot of it. Mostly diseases brought in by the white man.'

'I'm afraid,' said Hal, 'the white man has given these people a pretty raw deal.'

The doctor nodded. 'Spanish sailors brought tuberculosis to the islands about a hundred years ago. Forty years ago a German radio operator brought leprosy to Yap. English traders brought dysentery to Palau. Americans brought measles and other diseases far more serious. These people weren't used to such diseases. They died like flies. The population of Yap went down from 13,000 to 4,000. Kusaie had 2,000 natives before American whalers came roistering ashore – they were reduced to 200. The hundred thousand of the Mariana Islands were cut down to 3,000.'

'How many people are there in all your islands?'

'If you mean the 2,500 islands governed by the Navy as Trust Territory – the group called Micronesia – there are about 60,000 people. There used to be 400,000.'

'Are they still dying off?'

'No. The Japanese checked the decline. We have to give them credit. They had good doctors and hospitals. But I think we are doing even better. Because the population is increasing now on nearly all the islands.'

'It must give you a great lift,' Hal said, 'to feel that you're helping these people to get a new start.'

And he wished he were doing something like that. The collection and study of animals might be important, but it was cold business compared with helping your fellow man. What could he do for these islanders?

Of course the first and easiest thing he could do would be to take the missionary wherever he wanted to go. He would do that.

12 | To the secret atoll

FAR behind lay Ponape, its lofty Totolom Peak wrapped in a thunder cloud.

Everywhere else the sky was blue. The sea was calm and the motor-boat made good time. Dolphins played alongside. Flying-fish reflected the sunlight on their outspread fins.

The name of the boat, *Kiku*, was lettered on the bow in Japanese characters. Kiku meant Chrysanthemum.

Perhaps when the boat had been built in Japan it had been as beautiful as a flower and may even have smelled as sweet. But not now. It had a strong odour of dead-and-gone fish. Its decks and gunwales were scratched by the fins of countless bonitos, the daggers of swordfish and barracuda, and the sandpaper-rough skins of sharks.

But everyone aboard was happy. Omo in the galley hummed a Polynesian chant. Roger at the tip of the bow tried to catch flying-fish in his hands. Hal at the wheel basked in the tropical sunshine tempered by the cool ocean breeze.

But happiest of all hands was the Reverend Archibald Jones. Every few moments without any apparent reason he would break into a hearty roar of laughter.

'You're feeling pretty good,' commented Hal.

The missionary laughed until the tears came to his eyes. 'Oh, it's rich, it's rich! Imagine! *You* taking me right where I want to go....' He checked himself. 'I mean, my boy, it does my soul good. Your generosity has restored my faith in human nature. Yes, in the words of Holy Writ, it "hath put a new song in my mouth".'

'It's nothing,' Hal said.

'Oh yes it is. You have no idea what it means to me. No idea. Ha ha! Ahem! To think of being on my way at last to – to my chosen work among brown sheep that have gone astray. No wonder I feel like making a joyful noise unto the Lord.'

Strange talk, Hal thought. Somehow the Scriptures seemed dragged in by the heels. And the joyful noise of his curious passenger seemed to have more of the devil than the Lord in it.

But Hal did not consider himself a judge of such matters. His acquaintance with clergymen had been limited. Perhaps they all acted this way, he did not know.

What of it? How Mr Jones chose to talk was no business of his. His good deed was to land the holy man on some inhabited island where he could help the natives. The chart showed two such islands on the way to Pearl Lagoon.

By noon all of Ponape, including its cap of thunder, had sunk below the horizon. There was not a scrap of land to be seen anywhere. There was not a sail, not a wisp of steamer smoke. There was nothing to show where they had come from or where they were going – nothing but the compass and Hal's calculations.

'I hope you're a good navigator,' Roger said.

Hal got out the sextant and chronometer he had borrowed from the ship and took an observation. He entered the reading in the logbook. He set his course north by northwest. That ought to head him straight for Pearl Lagoon.

But he knew it would not be as simple as that. Winds would throw the *Kiku* off her course. Besides, they were now getting into the fringe of the North Equatorial Current. They had no way of judging its strength or exact direction. Its main trend was westward.

And to hit a tiny pinpoint of an island on the nose in this vast expanse of waters was a task that made Hal feel weak in the joints. The boat seemed so small and lost in this mightiest of oceans with the limitless sky above and, according to the chart, three miles of water between the keel and the hills and valleys of the sea bottom.

Hal checked his observations frequently, entering each new reading in the logbook. When night came the skies luckily remained clear and it was possible to steer by the stars. Omo and Roger relieved him at the wheel. Mr Jones was quite evidently not a sailor and spent the night comfortably in his bunk.

At sunrise the sea had humped itself a bit and the boat was rolling. Omo prepared a good breakfast and they sat down on the deck to eat it. Mr Jones finished first and with the plea that he was feeling a little seasick retired to the cabin.

A few moments later Hal went to the cabin to get the logbook. He found Mr Jones leaning over the open book and copying the readings on a slip of paper.

His back was partly towards Hal. It was curved like a barrel. Suddenly aware that someone was behind him, he hunched his back still more to cover his action and slipped the piece of paper into an inner pocket of his jacket.

Then he said cheerfully, 'I was just glancing over your log. Very interesting. I hope you don't mind.'

'Not at all,' said Hal, but he was staring. Staring at that back. It was still hunched as if concealing something. Where had he seen a back like that? A back with a secret. A back hiding a sneak.

Then he remembered. A back hunched just like this one, hunched as if over a secret. The back of the man who had come furtively from the house next to Professor Stuyvesant's. The man who had stepped into the black car. The car that Hal had suspected of following his into the country.

It was not much to go on, a slight hunch in a back. But now, with this copying of the log and quick concealment of the slip of paper, things began to add up. The professor had feared that his room was wired and their conversation

overheard. So he had not breathed aloud the bearings of the
island. That was the one bit of information the enemy must
get. And so this 'missionary', who was probably not a
missionary at all, had cleverly arranged to be taken straight
to the secret island. And by the bearings in the log he would
know exactly where it was and how to get there whenever
he wished to come again.

Hal went back on deck, took the wheel from Roger, and
began to think his way out of this one. He felt like kicking
himself for having been so easy. Welfare of the natives
indeed!

He knew he was up against a master, perhaps a mur-
derer, a man who would stop at nothing in his ambition to
acquire a fortune in pearls.

'What are you sweating about?' asked Roger, seeing the
beads of perspiration pouring down Hal's face. 'I'm as cool
as a cucumber.'

He would let Roger stay as cool as a cucumber for a
while. No need to worry him yet. Perhaps, thought Hal, his
own fears were groundless and the man was exactly what
he claimed to be.

And if he were not, he must not be allowed to know that
he was suspected. In that case he might take violent
measures. It was better to let him think that his scheme was
succeeding. If Roger and Omo shared Hal's fears they
might by a word or a look tip off the passenger to the fact
that he was under suspicion.

'I'll have to watch myself,' Hal thought. He must give no
hint that he smelled a rat. He must appear to be on the best
of terms with his now unwelcome guest. At the same time,
he must find a way to outwit him.

He puzzled and sweated over this problem for hours. But
when he took his next reading an answer suddenly came to
him.

He calculated the boat's position at 158° 15′ east by 8°
40′ north. But in entering the position in the log he sub-

tracted 10′ from each bearing. Thus according to the log the
reading was 158° 5′ east by 8° 30′ north.

At the next observation he subtracted twenty minutes
from each bearing, at the next thirty, at the next forty, and
so on. Thus the error on the page of the log grew rapidly
worse. But Hal, by simply adding the tens he had subtracted, always knew his true position.

He was not content with a noon sight, but took observations half a dozen times a day, because the chart indicated
the prevalence of hidden reefs.

He left the logbook in the cabin and gave Mr Jones
plenty of opportunity to consult it and copy the readings.

One minute of latitude was equal to a nautical mile, a bit
more than six thousand feet. So an error of ten minutes
meant the bearing was ten miles off. It would take only a
few such errors to put an island so far off course that it
could not be seen even from the masthead of a pearling
lugger.

If this man were a pearl thief, his plan doubtless was,
after learning the bearings of the island, to come back to it
with a pearling lugger and divers and help himself. Hal was
trying to make sure that he would never again find the
island. With such inaccurate bearings there was as much
chance of locating it as of finding a needle in a haystack.

The next day a few palms poked their heads over the
horizon and an island climbed up after them. Hal knew
from his readings that it could not be Pearl Lagoon but the
big passenger's eyes glowed with anticipation.

'This is perhaps your destination?' he asked.

'No,' said Hal. 'But perhaps you would like to be landed
here. Judging from the number of canoes along the shore,
there are plenty of natives here for you to minister to.'

But Mr Jones was not interested. 'I think I shall go a
little farther afield. Probably this island is served from
Ponape. My call is to virgin territory where the Bread of
Life has never been broken.'

Another island was sighted during the afternoon. But Mr Jones, learning that this too was not the goal of the *Kiku*, decided to continue.

Hal noticed that as they got farther from Ponape the chart grew less accurate. Some islands were marked with a P.D., meaning Position Doubtful. Islets appeared in the sea that were not on the chart and some on the chart were not to be found on the sea. Evidently the chart-makers were forced to indulge in a great deal of guesswork in regard to this almost unknown part of the Pacific.

It was a good place to get lost, Hal reflected. His head buzzed with the mathematical difficulties of computing his observations, allowing for semi-diameter, parallax, refraction, dip of the horizon, and all that. He felt very green. If he managed to compute his way to that pinpoint called Pearl Lagoon, it would be a miracle.

Always the bearings of Pearl Lagoon drummed in his mind – bearings he had never written down – 158° 12′ east by 11° 34′ north.

It went through his mind so automatically that he feared he would repeat it aloud in his sleep. If Mr Jones in his bunk only four feet from Hal should hear it, the jig would be up.

Another night of sailing under the bright stars. A little after sunrise Roger at the wheel shouted, 'Land-ho!'

'This is it,' thought Hal, tumbling out of his bunk. He came out on deck. The missionary lost no time in joining him.

Ahead lay a ring of reef enclosing a green lagoon. At two places the reef broadened to make islands but there was not much growing on them. Signs of the hurricane had been seen on some of the other islands the day before. This place had evidently been hit hard. Palm trees had been snapped off within ten feet of the ground. Only the stumps remained.

Hal excitedly took an observation. What if he had missed the right island entirely? But the reading when he worked it out was the same as the singsong that kept going through his brain – 158° 12′ east by 11° 34′ north.

This was Pearl Lagoon!

He sliced off ninety minutes from each bearing and wrote in the logbook: 'Sighted Pearl Lagoon at 156° 42′ east by 10° 4′ north.'

Let him copy that, he grinned. If his enemy ever chose to sail to that spot, he would find no island or, if he did, it would not be this one. He would be ninety miles west of the correct position and about the same distance south. That would put him more than a hundred miles from Pearl Lagoon.

Hal was thankful that Mr Jones was no sailor. The way he walked about the deck showed that. He lost his appetite when the sea was rough. He had occasionally operated the engine controls and held the wheel, but any amateur could do that. The only time he had tried the sextant he had held it upside down and he had never made any attempt to compute position by the *Nautical Almanac*. He was entirely at the mercy of Hal's figures.

All right, let him take a good look at Pearl Lagoon. He would never see it again.

'Let's circle it,' Hal said to Roger who was still at the wheel. 'Don't go too close to the reef.'

The atoll was less than a mile around. On the west side there was a good passage into the lagoon. Roger sped the boat through it upon the breast of an ocean swell. The water shoaled to a depth of only a fathom or two. The lagoon bottom seen through the clear green water was a paradise of coral castles of all the colours of the rainbow.

It was pitiful, the contrast between the beauty of the landscape underneath and the desolation of the hurricane-swept reef and its two battered islets.

'Certainly wouldn't like to be cast away here,' shivered Roger. 'Looks as if that storm didn't leave a thing alive. I'll bet it even killed the rats. Pearl Lagoon, eh? It ought to be

called Starvation Island.'

At a sign from Hal, Omo dropped anchor. Hal had selected the spot with some care. It was behind a high shoulder of reef which cut off the view of the northern part of the lagoon. The boat drifted to within a few feet of the reef where it was checked by the anchor chain.

'We're going ashore for a little while,' Hal said to Mr Jones. 'You probably won't be interested in this island because it's uninhabited. Perhaps you'll prefer to stay on board.'

Mr Jones pretended to welcome the suggestion. 'Yes, yes,' he said. 'I'll stay here. The place means nothing to me since there is no flock awaiting a shepherd.'

Hal, Roger, and Omo went over the side into water less than a foot deep and waded ashore. They clambered through humps of coral to the top of the reef and trudged northward. A shoulder of the reef soon cut them off from the view of the man in the boat.

13 | Pearl lagoon

UP the west reef they walked to where it broadened into an island at the north-west corner of the lagoon. Then there was a narrow neck of reef to another island at the north-east corner.

'It must be here somewhere,' said Hal. 'Professor Stuyvesant said the north-east corner.'

The island was only a few hundred yards across. The shrubbery, if there had ever been any, had been ripped away by the storm. Probably the whole island had been under water. The forlorn stumps of palm trees looked like monuments in a cemetery. A few palm logs remained – the rest had evidently been swept away.

It was hard going. The storm had left the surface a litter of coral blocks in piles sometimes ten feet high. If you stumbled and put out a hand it was cut by the sharp coral.

On the lagoon side of the island was a deep bay. It was not possible to see the bottom clearly for it was some ten fathoms down. The bay was a hundred yards across. The boys gazed down into its mysterious depths.

'Lucky we brought Omo,' Roger said. 'I could never get down that deep. How about you, Hal?'

'I wouldn't want to try it,' Hal said.

Omo made ready to slip off his dungarees but Hal stopped him. 'Wait a minute. Let's sit down and talk things over. Sort of a council of war.'

He told them his suspicions regarding the missionary.

'Perhaps you're right,' Omo said. 'I've known a lot of missionaries. He doesn't quite ring true.'

'I think he's a phony,' Roger said. 'Let's tell him so to his face.'

'Not unless we have to,' Hal warned. 'He's probably armed and we're not.'

'But he wouldn't kill us – just for some pearls.'

'Don't be too sure. There may be a fortune in this bay. I don't think he would stop at killing to get his hands on it. Remember, this isn't home – with a police station every few blocks. Here the law is whatever a man chooses to make it. Unless he forces our hand, let's just go along as usual. But I thought you ought to know so that if anything breaks we'll be prepared to act fast. Okay, Omo. Suppose you take a look at the bottom of this bay.'

Omo slid out of his clothes. Straight and strong and brown as the trunk of a coconut tree he stood poised on a rock overhanging the bay. His bathing-suit consisted solely of a pair of gloves. They would protect his hands when he seized the rough coral at the bottom to hold himself down or gripped the thorny oyster shells.

He began to go through the process that skin divers call 'taking the wind'. He breathed heavily, each breath deeper than the last, groaning and straining to force the air down. He pressed his diaphragm downwards with both hands to increase his capacity. He pumped the air into his lungs as if they were a compressor, and held it.

Then he dropped into the water. He did not dive but went straight down feet first without a splash.

The momentum took him to a depth of about ten feet. Then he turned end for end and swam downwards with powerful pulls of his arms and thrusts of his legs.

Hal and Roger had seen exhibitions of underwater swimming and had taken part in some of them. But they had never seen anything like this. Any American or European swimmer who could plough his way down to a depth of thirty feet was a champion. At that depth the pressure was tremendous. The water beneath seemed to be trying to throw you up like a cork exploding from a bottle.

But Omo went on down, to forty feet, fifty feet, sixty feet.

'And I'll bet he could go twice as deep as that if he had

to,' Hal said. 'These fellows really know how to swim. They learn before they are two years old. Lots of Polynesian babies can swim before they can walk. They're as much at home in water as on land – amphibians like the seals, turtles, frogs, and beavers.'

Now the boys could dimly see that Omo had stopped swimming. He was clinging to the coral bottom, his feet floating upward. He pulled himself down, let go, and took another hold a little farther on. He did this several times. He looked as if he were walking about the ocean floor on his hands.

Then he gripped something black and round and shot to the surface. He bobbed up out of the water waist high, sank back, came up again until his head was free, and clung to the rocks.

The compressed air came out of his lungs with a noise like the hiss of a piston. He breathed great gulps of pure air. His face was agonized and he did not seem to hear what the boys were saying.

Gradually his features relaxed. He looked up and smiled. The boys lent a hand as he clambered out of the water. He laid the black round thing on the rocks.

It was an enormous oyster fully fifteen inches across.

Roger shouted with glee. Hal silently thanked his lucky stars that he had found the right island, found the right bay, found the professor's oyster bed. This must be it, for the few oysters that grew wild in Micronesian waters were seldom more than six or eight inches in diameter.

'Are there many more like this?' Hal asked.

Omo nodded solemnly. 'That's why the bottom looks black. It's covered solid with shells. Hundreds of them.'

Roger danced with excitement. 'That means hundreds of pearls.'

'No,' Omo said quietly. 'Not every oyster produces a pearl. In fact we may have to open hundreds to get one.'

'That's usually the way of it,' Hal agreed. 'But here the

average may be higher because the professor has taken special pains to make favourable conditions.'

'There might be a pearl in this one.' Roger took out his sheath knife and tried to prise open the bivalve. He strained and sweated but it defied all his efforts.

'There's a little knack to it,' Omo said, and took the knife. Instead of prising, he thrust the knife between the lips of the shell, deep into the central closing muscle. With the muscle cut, the shell sprang open.

Then he let Roger take over. 'If there's a pearl,' he said, 'you'll probably find it by running your finger along the inside of the lip.'

Roger feverishly explored the inner edge of each shell. There was no pearl. Roger looked crestfallen. But he would not give up yet. 'There might be one inside.' He opened the shell completely and probed about in the oozy, sticky mass. He found nothing.

'What a mess!' he said disgustedly, and flung it behind him over a pile of coral blocks. It came down on the other side and hit something with a splash – and what sounded like a grunt. Roger darted behind the pile and encountered the Reverend Mr Jones wiping oyster out of his eyes, nose, and mouth.

He began to growl some remarks that did not sound well coming from a missionary. Then he remembered himself and tried to smile.

'What are you doing here?' demanded Roger.

The missionary did not deign to reply to this juvenile impertinence, but came around the pile to greet Hal and Omo. Oyster juice dripped from his ears.

'I was a little anxious about you,' he said, 'so I came to see if all was well.'

'You were spying on us!' Roger said hotly.

Mr Jones looked tolerantly at Roger. 'My boy, you must try to remember that good manners are next to godliness.'

'It's cleanliness that's next to godliness,' Roger corrected.

'And you'd better wash the oyster off your face.'

Mr Jones turned to Hal with a grieved air.

'Do you stand idly by while your brother flings insults as the gamin of an earlier day hurled stones at St Stephen? Is it not your duty as elder brother . . .'

'My duty as his elder brother,' Hall said, 'is to protect him from such scum as you. He was right – you were spying on us.'

'My son, you are overwrought. Your words are the hot irresponsible words of youth, but I would be a poor missionary indeed if I could not find it in my heart to forgive you,' and he put his hand on Hal's shoulder.

Hal shook it off. 'Cut that high-toned talk. You're no more a missionary than I am. You're a dirty two-faced crook.'

'Now, now,' said the missionary patiently, 'let's try to control ourselves. Tell me quietly what has given rise to this unfortunate misunderstanding.'

Hal was seized by doubt. Was he wrong after all? Certainly this man was showing a patience and forbearance worthy of any missionary.

He tried a new tack. 'Can you stand there and tell me you never heard of Professor Richard Stuyvesant?'

Mr Jones seemed to search his memory. 'Stuyvesant, Stuyvesant,' he mused. 'No, I can't say that the name is familiar to me.'

'And you didn't wire his laboratory?' persisted Hal. 'You didn't listen in on his conversations? You didn't overhear when he commissioned us to come to this island? You didn't come out of the next house and get into a black sedan? You didn't follow us to the Hunt Animal Farm?'

'I don't know what you are talking about,' said Mr Jones, but his voice had lost some of its assurance. A gob of oyster pulp dripped from the end of his long nose.

'And I suppose you didn't put Crab on the *Lively Lady* to get the bearings? He didn't go through my papers? You didn't wangle this trip with us so you could get our secret? Haven't you been copying the log? Did you get off on an island where you could preach to the natives? Not you. You don't care a hoot about the natives. You're interested in pearls.'

Mr Jones sat down heavily upon a palm log. He spread out his hands. His big shoulders were hunched forward. His face was dark with anger but he controlled himself.

'Well,' he said, 'I see the game is up. You've got it pretty well figured out, haven't you? I'm afraid you're too smart for me.'

Hal eyed him suspiciously. Was the fellow soft-soaping him to throw him off his guard?

'Yes,' went on Mr Jones, 'I see it's no use trying to pull the wool over your eyes. I should work with you, not against you.'

'There's no way you can work with us.'

'I'm not so sure of that, my friend. It's true I am not a missionary. That was just a playful deceit. I meant no harm.'

'You meant only to steal this pearl bed.'

'Don't say steal.' The big fellow brushed away the unpleasant word. 'I don't understand that this pearl bed belongs to anyone. This island isn't the professor's property. It doesn't even belong to the United States Government. It's part of a trusteeship under the United Nations – but even the United Nations doesn't claim to own it. It's nobody's – it's everybody's. And I'm part of everybody. So are you. This lagoon and anything that happens to be in it is common property. You and I have a right to it.'

'You mean to say that after all the trouble and expense the professor went to to plant this bed ...'

'The professor was a fool. He had too much faith in human nature. Well, it's human nature to look after yourself, and that's just what I'm doing. Now I'll be frank with you. My name is Merlin Kaggs. I'm a pearl trader. I buy pearls from the diving outfits in the South Seas and take them to New York and London and Paris and sell them. I know pearls. You could do worse than to go in with me. I can get prices for pearls that an amateur in the business couldn't possibly match. And I'm willing to share with you fifty-fifty. How does that sound?'

'If you will stand up,' Hal said evenly, 'I'll tell you how it sounds.'

The big man rose. Although Hal was six feet tall, Kaggs loomed over him like a Kodiak bear standing on its hind feet. Hal swung his right fist with all his might into the oyster-slippery face above him.

Kaggs staggered backwards a few steps. He did not return the blow. His right hand crept upward under his jacket to his left shoulder and came out holding a gun.

'You know so much about me,' Kaggs said thickly. 'Perhaps you don't know I've killed a man for less than that.'

'There's nothing to stop you from repeating the performance.'

Kaggs' eyes blazed. 'Any more lip from you and I will. Sit down with your back to that palm log. Be quick about it! And your brother beside you. Snap into it!'

Roger looked doubtfully at his brother. Hal did not move. But both of them came suddenly to life when the gun roared. Kaggs fired two shots, one of them barely missing Hal and the other coming within a few inches of Roger. The bullets ricocheted on the rocks and went spinning off towards the ocean. The report echoed back from the reef across the lagoon. A lone gull rose from a palm stump and flew off.

The two boys thought it best to sit where they were told.

'You wouldn't consider putting down that gun and fighting this out man to man?' Hal suggested.

'Man to boy,' sneered Kaggs. 'I could break you apart with my two hands. But why take the trouble? I use my brains, not my muscles. If you had sense enough to do the same you'd come in with me on this deal. But since you won't, I know who will. Omo, come over here.'

'You won't make any deal with Omo,' Hal said.

Kaggs laughed harshly. 'I never knew a native yet who couldn't be bought. Omo, I want you to dive for me. Right now. I'll pay you better than you were ever paid in your life. All right, get moving! Into the water!'

A slow smile came over Omo's handsome face. 'You are making a mistake, Mr. Kaggs,' he said politely. 'Perhaps your New Guinea savages can be bought, but not a man of Raiatea.'

'You'll do what this gun tells you to do. Get going or I'll smear you all over the rocks.'

Omo glanced at Hal, then back at Kaggs.

'How much will you pay me?'

'Now you're talking sense. I'll pay you a fifth of all you bring up, shell or pearls.'

Omo nodded thoughtfully. 'My gloves,' he said. 'They're on that rock behind you, Mr Kaggs.'

Kaggs turned to get the gloves and Hal half-rose. Kaggs swung back to cover him with the gun.

'Get them yourself,' he told Omo.

Omo passed behind him. Kaggs turned sidewise and kept a watchful eye on all three of his antagonists.

Hal made a quick move that attracted Kaggs' attention and at the same instant Omo bounded like a tiger upon the big man's shoulders. He locked an arm about his neck. As Kaggs' gun hand came up Omo seized the wrist and tried to squeeze the gun loose. Hal and Roger were attacking from in front.

Kaggs, straining every nerve, kept his grip on the gun and turned its muzzle to bear upon Hal.

'Look out! The gun!' Omo cried. He vainly struggled to twist the arm that held it. The gun blazed. The pearl trader's previous shots had been warnings only, but this time he meant business. Only the Polynesian's tugging on his wrist prevented the shot from reaching its mark.

Again he brought the gun to bear on Hal whose fists were methodically crashing into his face.

Omo despaired of controlling that powerful arm. But there was one thing left that he could do. He swung around his opponent's shoulder so that he came between the gun and Hal. There was a shot and Omo fell to the ground.

Hal immediately dropped beside his friend. Vividly he remembered the night on the beach at Bikini when they had sworn loyalty to each other and had exchanged names. Omo had been true to his pledge.

Roger quit his pummelling of the giant's solar plexus to see what had happened to Omo. Kaggs promptly disappeared.

'Let him go,' Hal said. He wouldn't leave Omo now. 'We'll deal with him later.'

Omo lay with eyes closed. Hal felt his pulse. It was still beating. Blood trickled from his right leg some ten inches above the knee.

Hal examined the wound. There were two holes, one where the bullet had gone in, one where it had come out. The skin about the first hole was scorched with powder burns because of the close range of the firing.

The bullet had probably gone through a muscle. Luckily it had missed the artery. The wound was bleeding, but not profusely.

Hal stripped off his shirt, soaked it in the lagoon, and bathed the wound.

'Wish we had some penicillin,' he said, 'or some sulfa powder.'

'We've got both on the boat,' Roger said. 'Shall I go and get them?'

'We could take care of him better on board. Put him in his bunk. But it would be pretty hard to carry him over this rough ground. Suppose you run the boat over here. No, wait a minute. I think I hear the motor now.'

Sure enough, across the lagoon came the gug-gug-gug of the *Kiku*'s engine.

'Kaggs is bringing it. The fellow must have a white streak in him after all.'

Out from behind an elbow of the reef came the *Kiku* and plodded its way across the lagoon and into the bay of pearls. Hal in the meantime had turned his shirt into a tourniquet and applied it just above the wound. He must remember to loosen it every fifteen minutes.

He could almost forgive Kaggs. Evidently the big fellow was sorry for what he had done.

'Show him where to bring the boat up against the rocks,' Hal called to Roger.

Then he looked up, surprised, for the motor had quit. The boat was still a hundred feet away from shore. She had almost lost momentum.

'You'll have to give her a little more to bring her up,' Hal called.

Kaggs' reply was a lazy laugh. He spun the wheel. The boat slowly turned and came to a standstill with her bow headed out towards the lagoon.

'You're making a slight mistake,' Kaggs chuckled. 'I wasn't planning to come ashore. Just wanted to exchange a few compliments with you before I leave.'

Hal and Roger stared, unbelieving.

'What do you mean, leave?' demanded Hal, uneasiness crawling like a snake along his backbone.

'Just what I say. You won't take me up on my proposition, so I'll have to go alone. I'll toddle down to Ponape and get a pearling lugger and divers. Then I'll be back.'

'You can't do it,' Hal said. 'You know you can't navigate.'

'What of it? Ponape is a big island. If I keep her headed south I'm pretty sure to strike it.'

'But Omo should be taken to a doctor. He may die here. Doesn't that concern you?'

'Why should it?'

'And this place...' Hal looked about him at the hurri-
cane-ruined island and panic shook him. 'You can't leave
us here. We couldn't last until you got back. There's no
food. I haven't even seen a crab. There's no shade, nothing
to make a hut out of. There's no water. We'd die of thirst.
And you'll go to prison.'

'I've been to prison,' Kaggs said. 'I don't plan to go
again. That's why I didn't shoot all three of you dead. If
anybody asks me – and I don't suppose anybody will – I'll
just say you decided to stay on the island till I come back.
If you can't stick it out it'll be no hair off my hide.'

His hand reached for the throttle.

'Wait!' called Hal. 'At least you can do this. Reach into
the first-aid kit and fling us that tube of penicillin and the
can of sulfa.'

Kaggs laughed. 'Might need them myself, old man. No
telling what might happen on the perilous deep you know.'

The light breeze had been drifting the boat a little closer
to shore. Suddenly Roger made a running dive into the cove
and swam for the boat with swift powerful strokes. In a
flash Hal was after him. If the motor failed to start at the
first touch they might just make it. Exactly what they could
do against an armed man when they got there they did not
stop to consider.

Kaggs slipped the throttle. The engine roared into life.
The propeller churned. The heavy boat got under way
slowly and it seemed for a moment that the boys would
overtake it. Then it began to pull away faster than they
could swim.

They stopped swimming and, treading water, watched
the boat chug away across the lagoon. Just before it
rounded the spur of rock that hid the channel to the ocean,
Kaggs waved his hand.

Then there was nothing to be seen but the wake of the
boat across the lagoon. And nothing to be heard but the cry

of the lone gull left by the hurricane.

'That's that,' said Hal, thus mildly expressing the despair that iced his heart. They wearily swam back to the shore, crawled out onto the hot rocks, and dropped beside Omo.

Hal and Roger stared at each other in silence. It was still hard to realize what had happened to them. Their eyes travelled over the bare piles of coral blocks.

Roger began to laugh weakly. 'I've always wanted to be cast away on a desert island. But I never meant it to be quite as much of a desert as this!'

14 | Desert island

OMO stirred and groaned. A wrinkle of pain went across his forehead. He opened his eyes. He looked up at Hal and Roger. Slowly he remembered what had happened.

'Sorry I passed out on you.' He tried to get up but sank back, making a wry face.

'Better lie still,' Hal said. Omo managed a grin. 'What's been going on while I've been snoozing? Have I missed something?'

'Not much. We've just been saying goodbye to Kaggs.'

'Goodbye?'

'He's gone – with the boat. To Ponape to get a lugger and divers.'

Now Omo's eyes opened wide. 'No! He must be bluffing – just trying to scare you into making a deal with him. He'll be back before night. He wouldn't leave us on this reef.'

'Wish I could think so.'

'But it would take him at least three days to get to Ponape. He might have to stay there a week or even two before he could get a lugger and divers – they're hard to come by. Then three or four days to come back. Does he realize what could happen to us in three weeks?'

'I think he does. But that doesn't worry him.'

'Or even one week,' said Omo, looking about at the desolation of white rocks under the blinding sun. 'Do you know why this island is uninhabited?'

'No – why?'

'Because men can't live here. Or, at least, none have been willing to try. There could never have been enough to support life here – and what little there was was smashed by the hurricane. Even the birds have no use for the place. I haven't seen any fish in the lagoon. Roger called it Starvation Island. That's a good name for it. Or Dead Man's Reef.'

He closed his eyes and wrestled for a while with pain. Then he looked up and smiled.

'I shouldn't talk that way. Guess it was just because I felt weak. Of course we can make a go of it – somehow. But there's a lot to do. I can't lie here taking my ease.' He struggled to a sitting position.

'You lie down!' said Hal sharply. 'Now see what you've done – started it bleeding again. And we don't have any medicine.'

'Luckily that's where you're wrong,' Omo said weakly. 'This is a medicine chest that I have my head on.' His head rested on a palm log.

'What can we do with that?'

'Take your knife, Hal, and scrape the bark. Scrape it fine so as to make a powder. Then put it on. It's astringent. It will stop the bleeding.'

'But is it antiseptic?'

'Oh yes. The sun has sterilized it.'

Hal had often heard of the skilful use the Polynesians make of herbs, grasses, roots, and trees for medical purposes, but had not expected to find a medicine chest under his patient's head.

He scraped until he had a plentiful supply of the powdered bark of the coconut palm and then applied it to the wound, binding it in place with a strip torn from his shirt which was serving as a tourniquet.

Hal put his hand on Omo's forehead. It was hot. Omo was tossing feverishly.

'We've got to get him into the shade,' Hal told Roger. Squinting to protect their eyes from the glare they scanned the island. The blazing rocks laughed back at them.

There was a band of shade cast by a palm stump. They

laid Omo in it. It was better than nothing, although as the
sun travelled across the sky they would have to keep shift-
ing the patient.

'Somehow we'll have to build a shelter,' Hal said.

Roger laughed bitterly. 'Fat chance!' But he got up at
once and began to search the island for building materials.

Omo was muttering and Hal bent down to hear what he
was saying.

'I hope that what I said didn't worry you, Hal. We can
manage all right. After all, it won't be long. A week or two,
or three, and he'll be back. He can find it okay – he's got
the log to go by. It isn't as if he weren't coming back. That
would be tough. No ships ever come by here. We could rot.
But there's no need to worry about that – he'll be back.'

'Yes, Omo,' Hal said. 'Now see if you can snatch some
sleep.'

A terrible chill settled upon Hal's heart. He alone knew
that Kaggs would never come back.

Kaggs had the log to go by. What a bitter joke that was!
Hal had intended it to be a joke on Kaggs. It had turned
into a joke on himself and his two companions. A joke that
might cost them their lives.

The bearings in the log were a hundred miles off. Finding
no island there, Kaggs would not have the slightest idea in
what direction to sail. The chances would be a thousand to
one, perhaps a million to one, against his finding Pearl
Lagoon. He might hunt for it for months, or years, without
success. He could come within a few miles of it without
seeing it. Nowhere did the reef rise more than ten feet
above sea level and there was not a tree left standing. At
a short distance the white reef might be mistaken for a
wind ripple on the ocean's surface.

And even if Kaggs did by a miracle come upon the island
after perhaps a year of search, what good would it do
them? He would find their white bones among the rocks.

Perhaps Kaggs had not actually meant them to die here.

Perhaps he had intended to get back before they perished. But Hal had fixed it so that he would not get back.

Would Roger and Omo blame him when they knew that he had signed their death warrants? They would try not to, but could they help it as they lay dying of starvation and thirst on this horrible white skeleton of coral rock?

At least he could not tell them yet. It might snuff out what little hope they had and endanger Omo's recovery.

Hal dismissed his gloomy thoughts and devoted himself to Omo. The wound had stopped bleeding. The native remedy had worked. He cautiously removed the tourniquet – it would be well to get it off to avoid any chance of gangrene. Still the wound did not bleed. Hal developed high respect for the astringent qualities of powdered coconut bark.

He took the torn shirt to the edge of the cove, soaked it, waved it in the air so that evaporation might cool the water in it, and laid it across Omo's hot forehead. Omo hardly seemed to know what was going on.

Roger was not having much luck. The natural material to make a roof would be palm leaves. There were numerous palm stumps, but most of the fallen trees had been washed away by the waves which had evidently rolled high across the reef during the storm.

A few of the logs had been pinned fast between the rocks. He examined them hopefully but their leaves had been stripped from them before they fell.

Well, it didn't have to be palm leaves. He shut his eyes, for the light was blinding, and tried to think what else he could use. Pandanus leaves would do, or taro leaves, or banana leaves. On a proper desert island there would be all of these and more. He had read many stories of castaways on desert islands. He knew just what a desert island ought to be.

It should be a jungle as full of food as a refrigerator. You had only to reach up and pluck a banana or a bread-fruit or

a wild orange or a lime or a mango or a papaya or a
custard apple or a durian or a persimmon or a mamey or a
guava or some wild grapes. The lagoon was full of fish, you
could dig up any quantity of clams and mussels from the
beaches, the birds were so plentiful you could catch them
by hand, there were nests full of eggs in the cliffs on the
seaward side, you could trap a great sea turtle when it
comes ashore at night to deposit its eggs, you could drink
pure water of mountain streams and bathe in woodland
pools – and you could make a house of bamboo poles and
palm thatch in no time.

He opened his eyes and the glare of the white rocks hit
him so hard that he blinked with pain.

Then he saw something lying among the rocks just above
the reach of the surf. It looked like a boat upside down.
Perhaps it *was* a boat tossed ashore by the storm.

His heart began to thud with excitement. If it was a boat
they could escape from Starvation Island. He ran towards
it, stumbling over the rough coral.

It was not a boat, but a great fish. It lay belly upward
and was quite dead. It was fully thirty feet long and as big
round as an elephant.

Its body was brownish and covered with white spots. Its
face was the ugliest Roger had ever seen. It looked like the
face of a very unhappy bullfrog enlarged many hundreds of
times. Far out at each corner popped out a small eye.

But the most terrific feature was the mouth. It was four
feet wide. Long fringes dropped from its corners.

One would think that such a huge and hideous creature
would be a cannibal and a man-eater, but Roger had
already had some acquaintance with fish of this sort. He
knew it to be a whale shark, the largest of all living fish,
sometimes twice as long as this specimen. Although a
shark, it was harmless and lived on very small creatures,
some of them so small that they could be seen only with a
microscope.

'But this isn't getting us a roof,' Roger reminded himself, and started away. Then a thought struck him and he turned back. He tried to remember pictures he had once seen of the houses of tribes living along the Amur River in Siberia. In that region there were no trees to use as building materials, so the men made their houses of – fishskins!

What was the matter with building a shanty out of sharkskin?

He ran back to tell Hal. He expected his brother to laugh at his idea but Hal said, 'Why not? I think you've got something there.'

They went back to the sea monster.

'That surely must be the plainest face in the whole Pacific Ocean,' Hal said. He touched the hard sandpapery skin. 'It's not going to be easy to cut that. But we have good knives. We'll slit him down the belly and then cut just behind the head and in front of the tail fin.'

The skin was as tough as emery cloth. Sometimes the knife could not be forced into it unless pounded in with a coral block.

Hal, sweating and straining, said, 'There's one good thing about it. Once we get it up it will be more durable than any roof of palm thatch. It ought to last as long as asbestos shingles!'

'And all we ask,' Roger put in, 'is for it to last a couple of weeks until Kaggs gets here.'

Hal felt his heart sink. He was not ready to tell Roger yet, but shouldn't he begin to prepare his mind for the bad news that Kaggs would not return?

'Of course,' and he tried to speak lightly, 'there's always a chance that we won't see him again.'

Roger stopped and looked at him.

'Then what will happen to us?'

'Oh, we'll make out. We'll have to. Now then, let's try to flay the skin up at this corner. Boy, isn't it thick!'

After two hours of hard work they stopped for breath.

The skin was not more than half off. The smell of the dead fish was overpowering. The sun beat down like hammers on their heads. Their eyes were narrowed to slits to avoid the glare. Roger wiped his perspiring face with his sleeve. Hal, having made a tourniquet, bandages, and a wet compress out of his own shirt, dried his face on his brother's shirt-tail.

'I could do with a drink of water,' Roger said.

Hal looked serious. 'What have I been thinking of? Water! That's more important than shelter – more important even than food. Let's leave the rest of this job until tomorrow. I'll see how Omo is – then we'll go on the trail after water.'

Omo was asleep. The shadow of the stump had left him. Hal and Roger moved him into the shade and Hal soaked the compress and replaced it on the patient's forehead.

The quest for water began. The boys started out in apparently good spirits but secretly each had little hope. How could one expect to find fresh water on this sunburnt reef?

'It must have rained a lot here during the hurricane,' Hal said. 'There may be some of it left in the hollows of rocks.'

Close to the shore a rock hollowed out like a bowl held a little water. Roger eagerly ran to it, scooped up a little of the water in his hand, and tasted it. He spat it out.

'Salty!'

'It must have been left there by the surf at high tide,' Hal guessed. 'Let's look farther away from the shore.'

They found plenty of hollowed rocks but no water in them. In some were lines showing that they had contained water but it had long since soaked away through the porous coral.

Roger surveyed the coconut stumps.

'There must have been nuts on these trees.'

If they could find them they would not lack for drink nor

for food. How refreshing the sweet, cool, milky water of the coconut would be! And the soft white meat!

A diligent search failed to discover any coconuts.

'The trouble with coconuts,' Hal said, 'is that they float. When the sea swept over the land it must have carried them all off.'

'What do we do next?' inquired Roger.

'Dig,' suggested Hal. He led the way to the lagoon beach. 'They say you can sometimes find fresh water if you dig a hole in the beach at low tide. How about this spot – just below the high-tide mark?'

'It sounds crazy to me,' Roger said, 'but mine not to question why, mine but to do or die,' and he picked up a flat piece of coral to use as a shovel and began to dig.

At a depth of about three feet Hal stopped. 'Quit digging. Let's see what happens now.'

Water began to ooze into the hole. Presently it was four or five inches deep.

'But what makes you think this will be fresh water?'

'I don't think so,' Hal said. 'I only hope so. It has happened on other atolls. Shipwrecked sailors have escaped dying of thirst by drinking the water from holes like this one.'

'But why would it be fresh?'

'The sea water filtering through the sand loses some of its salt. And then there's the rainwater that filters down through the rocks. Suppose you try it now. But be careful to skim off just the surface. The fresh water is lighter than sea water and lies on top.'

Roger scooped off a little of the surface water and tasted it. Then he gulped down a couple of handfuls. 'Salty,' he said, 'but not as bad as sea water.'

Hal tasted the warm brackish water. He was disappointed. 'It wouldn't take much of that to make you sick.'

Roger was gagging and holding his forehead. Presently he lost his breakfast.

He turned upon his brother angrily. 'You and your fresh water! What you don't know about how to survive on a desert island would fill a book.'

'I'm afraid you're right,' Hal admitted. 'All I know is that the U.S. Navy instructs survivors to do just what we have done.'

'Then why didn't it work?'

'Perhaps because the sand is too coarse here to filter out the salt. Or perhaps there wasn't enough rain, or it sank away through the rocks.'

'All right, don't stand there giving me perhapses. Find me some water.'

'Sometimes,' Hal said, 'I think you're a spoiled brat. Do you suppose you are the only thirsty person on this reef?'

Roger was silent. They resumed their dreary search. They walked across the narrow part of the reef where it stretched like a bridge from one island to the other. On one side the ocean surf splashed among the rocks. On the other side a white beach sloped to the blue lagoon. The lagoon was as smooth as glass. It was not more than a dozen feet deep here and the bottom was a fairy city of pink palaces, towers, pagodas, and minarets, all built by the tiny coral insects.

It was very lovely if you could just forget being hot, tired, sore-eyed, and thirsty. But you couldn't forget.

The reef broadened to form the other island. They spent an hour or more exploring it. There was no water, except surf water, in the cups of the rocks. There were coconut stumps and logs but no leaves. They looked hopefully in the tops of the stumps for pockets of rainwater, but it had dried away.

Then they found a coconut! It was pinned under a rock where the waves that had buried the island had failed to dislodge it.

Trembling with excitement, they slashed away the husk. The nut inside was cracked. Inserting his knife in the crack,

Hal prised off the cap of the nut. Both boys groaned when they saw the contents.

'Suffering cats!' Roger mourned. 'It's rotten!'

Salt water entering through the crack had spoiled both the meat and the liquid.

Hal scraped out the inside of the nut. 'At least we have a cup now.'

'What's the use of a cup with nothing to put in it?'

'We'll find something.'

They searched until the sun was low in the west. Their stomachs were now reminding them of the need for food as well as water.

'Here's water!' exclaimed Hal. Roger came to see what he had found. It was nothing but a low flat weed rooted in a little soil between the rocks.

'So that's water!' sneered Roger.

Hal paid no attention to his sarcasm. He broke off one of the small pulpy leaves and chewed it. The leaf was full of a cool juice. It was wonderfully refreshing to the dry mouth and parched tongue. A grin of content spread over Hal's face.

Roger bit into a leaf. 'Boy, does that taste good!' But he did not take any more. The two boys, with a single thought, dug up the plant and trudged with it to their own island. If they were thirsty, their feverish patient would be much more so.

Omo was tossing restlessly. He opened his eyes. They were bright with fever.

'We brought you some water, Omo. But it's water you have to chew. I don't know what your island name for it is, but we call it pigweed or purslane.'

Omo took the plant eagerly. He chewed the leaves, stems, and roots, extracting and swallowing the juice.

'It's wonderful,' he said gratefully. 'I hope you got plenty more for yourselves.' His eyes questioned Roger.

'Take it all,' Roger said. 'We're okay.'

'Sorry we can't offer you any dinner,' Hal said.

Omo smiled. 'Water was all I wanted. Now I can sleep,' and he closed his eyes.

Hal looked for more pigweed but found none. The drop or two of water he had pressed out of the leaf seemed only to have increased his thirst. He was glad to see the killer sun sink below the horizon. The coral rocks quickly lost their heat. Thank heaven for the night! He dreaded the thought that another blazing day must come, and another, and another, until they died in this infernal sea-trap.

How to get water! It was still the number one problem. He sat down to think. His hand rested upon a rock. Suddenly he realized that the rock was damp.

The dew! The dew was falling. In the darkening shadows a mist drifted over the lagoon. If he could find a way to catch the dew....

The Polynesians had a way of doing that. If he could just remember how it went. He would like to ask Omo – but Omo must be allowed to sleep.

He went to the lagoon beach and dug a shallow hole in the sand about two feet wide. He placed the cup of coconut shell at the bottom. He covered the hole with Roger's shirt taken from Omo's forehead. Omo would not need it now that the air was cool. He pierced an opening in the shirt just over the cup. Then he piled a pyramid of stones about three feet high over the shirt.

The principle of the thing was that dew would collect in the chinks between the stones, trickle through them to the shirt, and run down into the cup. In the morning there might be a cupful of fresh water.

Hal went back to find Roger stretched out on the rocks near Omo fast asleep. Hal tried to make himself comfortable on the lumpy coral.

But he could not sleep. The three words that separate life from death kept going through his brain – water, food, shelter.

He thought of the soft life at home. Where you slept in a smooth bed under a good roof. Where you had only to turn a tap to get water. Where you were called three times a day to a table groaning with food.

Life was so easy at home that a fellow got out of the habit of appreciating it. You took it for granted. Hal was certain he would never take it for granted again.

His throat was as dry as sandpaper and his stomach felt as hollow as a drum. He dozed off and dreamed of rain. He woke up with a start and looked at the sky.

There was not a cloud as big as his hand. The stars blazed like the hot merciless suns they were. The Milky Way looked like a path of powdered glass.

That other night on the island at Bikini he had heard small animals moving through the brush. Here on Dead Man's Reef, as Omo had called it, there was no sound but the sob and suck of the surf. There was even the smell of death, drifting across the island from the body of the rotting shark.

Hal fell into a troubled sleep.

15 | The sharkskin house

THE light of early dawn woke him. There were kinks and quirks in his back where the rocks had jabbed him with their sharp elbows. But the air was cool and fresh. Hal did not feel quite as hungry and thirsty as he had the night before. He knew that was not a good sign – his system was becoming numb.

The brisk invigorating air put new ambition into him. Somehow they were going to beat this reef, and Kaggs too.

He tried to remember how it went in the poem – the morning's dew-pearled, all's right with the world. He rose cheerfully and went to see what he had caught in his dew-trap.

The coconut shell was nearly half-full of water. He had hoped for more but evidently the dew had been light. He took the precious liquid to camp.

Omo was stirring but seemed to be in a sort of stupor. Hal raised his head and poured half of the water down his throat.

'You drink the rest,' he told Roger who was sitting up yawning, rubbing some of the creases out of his hide. Hal put the cup in Roger's hands and went off to renew his attack upon the sharkskin. That terrific sun would be rising soon and it was essential that they should have some protection against it.

Roger sat looking at the water in the bottom of the shell. If he had been offered a choice between the water and a hundred dollars at that moment he would have said, 'Me for the water!' But shucks! – camels could go a week without water. And his brother had called him a spoiled brat. Omo was groaning softly. He was muttering, 'It's so hot – so hot – so hot!' Perspiration ran down his face. If he was so hot before sunrise, how would he feel later? Roger parted Omo's lips and emptied the cup into the brown boy's mouth.

Then, feeling pretty noble, he went to join Hal. He wanted to tell Hal what he had done so that his brother wouldn't think him a spoiled brat. But he decided to hold his tongue.

The red-hot devil of a sun rose before they finished flensing off the skin. It was a magnificent sheet nearly twenty feet long and eight wide. They scraped the fat off the inner surface. Then they stood back and admired their work.

'That was a good idea of yours,' Hal said.

'Well, I remembered your telling me that somewhere they build houses of fishskin. Isn't it in Siberia?'

'Yes. The people called the Fishskin Tartars. Their food is fish, they make their clothes and shoes out of fishskin, and their huts are built of poles with fishskin stretched over them. And you can always tell when you come near a fishskin village by the smell!'

'I know what you mean,' said Roger, turning up his nose.

'The sharkskin won't smell so bad after the sun has cured it. But we ought to get rid of the carcass. Let's try to roll it down where high tide will take it.'

By dint of hard labour they inched the monster's body down close to the water's edge.

'There's a lot of meat here,' Roger said. 'It's a shame we can't eat it.'

'It's too badly decayed. Better to eat nothing than that.'

So, turning their backs upon the poisonous breakfast that the sea had offered them, they returned to camp, dragging the sharkskin behind them.

Now they launched into building operations in earnest. Having no nails, screws, or bolts, no beams, joists, or planks, nothing that a house-builder would ordinarily think necessary, they had to use considerable ingenuity.

'We have only enough skin for the roof,' Roger said. 'How about piling up rocks to make the walls?'

'Sure! But we'll need a ridgepole. And a couple of posts to hold it up. That palm log might do for a ridgepole. It's slender – I think we can lift it.'

'And if we could find a couple of stumps the right distance apart they would do for posts.'

There were plenty of palm stumps left standing. They found two that stood about eight feet high and a dozen feet apart. With their knives they cut notches in the tops of the stumps and hoisted the palm log in place so that it lay in the notches and stretched from one stump to the other. Now they had their ridgepole.

'Funny to start with the roof,' Roger said.

'Not so funny. The Polynesians often do that, and the Japanese always do. Build the roof first, hoist it up on stilts, hold a celebration, and then build the house under the roof.'

They stretched the twenty-foot skin over the ridgepole so that it was ten feet long on each side. Then they proceeded to build the walls. They piled coral blocks up to a height of about four feet. They fitted them together as well as possible so that the inside surface would be nearly vertical. On the outside the wall was solidly buttressed with more rocks. They left four gaps to serve as doors for getting in and out, and for ventilation.

Then they stretched the sharkskin out until it went smooth and straight from the ridgepole in both directions down to the tops of the walls. There they pinned it fast with lumps of coral.

The house was finished – and surely no stranger one had ever been seen, even in the land of the Fishskin Tartars!

They brought Omo in and laid him down on the least rough portion of the coral floor. He breathed a sigh of contentment for the place was dark and cool. The three-foot-thick rock walls defied the sun. The sharkskin, although not as heatproof as palm thatch, was thicker than shingles. The roof was a bit low, but it was better to have it low and snug in case of a windstorm.

The room measured only eight feet in the direction of the ridgepole, but nearly twenty feet the other way – quite big enough for three persons.

'There's even room enough to do our cooking inside on rainy days,' Hal said.

'*If* there is any rain. And *if* we have anything to cook. And *if* we can make a fire without matches.'

Hal gritted his teeth. 'We've got to lick those ifs. We can't make it rain, but there must be some way to find fresh water. Let me think. You can get water from the *guiji* vine but none of it grows here. There's water in the barrel cactus but there's no barrel cactus. How about pandanus? It often grows even in as bad a spot as this. Those little air roots that look like leaves contain water. Let's go.'

They went out with pretended enthusiasm but no real expectation of finding pandanus.

Hal picked up a pebble and gave it to Roger. 'Chew on

that,' he suggested. 'It makes the saliva flow and you'll almost think you're getting a drink.'

They searched diligently the rest of the day. They found no pandanus nor anything else that yielded moisture. This reef seemed as dead and dry as the moon.

At night Hal again built a cairn of stones to collect dew. But a wind came up and dew did not form. In the morning the cup was empty. Even the patient had to go without water.

Omo was conscious now. His leg gave him great pain and he suffered from thirst that had been made more intense by his fever. But the heat had gone from his forehead and cheeks. Hal consulted him on the problem of water. He told him what they had done to find it. 'You probably would have better ideas.'

'No, I would have done just what you have done. You were pretty smart – that pigweed and then catching the dew.'

'I never felt so stupid in my life,' Hal grumbled.

Omo looked at his friend's haggard and troubled face.

'You're letting worry get you down. Will you do me a favour?'

'Sure. Anything.'

'You and Roger go in for a swim. Our people believe that when things get very bad it helps to turn your back on them and go and play for a while. It will relax you. You'll be able to think better.'

'Very well, Dr Omo, if you insist,' Hal said. 'But it seems an awful waste of time.'

'Boy, it sounds good to me,' Roger said. 'Let's go in on the ocean side – it will be cooler.'

They plunged into the surf. The bottom did not slope gradually away but dropped abruptly to great depths. They performed like two playful seals, diving, swimming, splashing, and their cares flowed away like raindrops from a duck's back.

'You can't catch me,' shouted Roger.

'What'll you bet?'

'I'll betcha this island.'

'I don't want your blasted island, but I'll catch you,' and Hal burrowed deep down after the disappearing form of Roger.

At a depth of twenty feet or more. Roger began following the shore. Hal was close behind. Where the bridge of reef widened into the second island Roger suddenly felt the water go very cold.

It seemed to be a submarine current coming from the land. In a moment he was out of it. Now Hal felt it. Astonished, both boys popped to the surface.

Roger shook the water from his face. 'What do you make of that?'

'It comes from a cave in the land. Do you know what that means?'

'Can't say that I do.'

'It means it's fresh water, or I'm a donkey's breakfast.'

'You're probably a donkey's breakfast,' agreed Roger.

'Wish we had a bottle. Well, let's go down and fill our mouths.'

Hal dived. When his head came into the cold stream he opened his mouth and let the water crowd in. It was fresh and sweet! He swallowed it, gulped another mouthful, and came up. Roger emerged beside him.

'It's the real thing,' he marvelled.

Hal was beaming. 'Things are looking up,' he exulted. 'Stay here and mark the place while I get the cup.'

In ten minutes he was back with the coconut shell.

'But it ought to have a lid or a cork,' Roger said. 'How can you keep it empty until you get down there?'

'I don't think it needs to be empty.' And Hal dived with the shell which promptly filled with sea-water. When he reached the cold stream he held the cup in it and turned it upside down. He pushed his hand into it a few times to change the water. The salt water, being heavier, should fall out of the cup and be replaced by fresh.

He turned the shell right side up and rose to the surface. He joined Roger on the rocks.

'Try it.' He offered the cup to Roger who warily tasted the liquid. Then he began to gulp it down greedily.

'Go easy!' warned Hal. 'You're as dry as a bone inside. You'll have trouble if you take on too much all at once.'

Refilling the cup at the submarine spring, they carried the precious liquid to Omo. When the fever-worn patient saw the cup full of water, tears came to his eyes. He took one sip, then put the cup aside.

'I've never tasted anything so good in all my life.'

'Won't you have more?' Hal asked.

'Later. My stomach isn't used to such luxury.'

'Now we have two of the necessities of life,' Hal said, 'shelter and water. But my insides tell me that we can't keep going much longer without food.'

Omo groaned. 'I ought to be helping you. And here I am lying flat on my back as useless as a log.'

Hal looked affectionately at his brown companion. 'You were mighty useful to me when you stopped that bullet.'

'Forget it.'

'I'll never forget it. Perhaps I can pay you back some day. Just at the moment the best thing I can do for you is to get you something to eat. Come on, Roger.'

Roger hated to leave the cool shade of the sharkskin cave.

'I don't believe there's a mouthful of food on this infernal reef,' he grumbled.

'There's one good sign,' Omo said, 'that gull that you say is on the island. He wouldn't stay if there weren't anything to eat.'

'I'm sorry to report,' Hal said, 'that he's gone. He flew away last night.'

For a moment no one spoke. In spite of the water, de-

spair lay heavy upon their spirits. Hunger made them feel
weak and hopeless. Hal roused himself. He sprang up, not
very briskly for his legs felt uncertain, and started out of
the hut.

'Come on, old man,' he called back to Roger. 'We're
going to show that gull he made a mistake!'

16 | The castaways eat

HUNGER sharpened their eyes. They went over the reef with a fine-tooth comb. Nothing was too small to escape their attention.

They turned over rocks and looked beneath. They moved logs. They burrowed in the sand of the beach.

It was most disappointing.

After three hours of it, Roger dropped wearily to the ground with his head against a log. He felt as if he never wanted to move again.

Gradually he became aware of a scratching sound. It seemed to be inside the log. He called Hal.

'Put your ear against this log. Do you hear anything?'

Hal listened. 'There's something alive in there. Perhaps we can get at it with our knives.'

They cut into the log which proved to be decayed. Presently Roger gave a grunt of disgust. He had uncovered something that looked like a fat caterpillar.

'It's a grub!' exclaimed Hal. 'Later on it changes into the white beetle. Put it in your pocket and let's see if there're any more of them.'

'You don't mean to say we're going to eat them!'

'Of course we are! Beggars can't be choosers.'

They found fourteen of the grubs and took them to show to Omo.

'Aren't they poison?' Roger asked doubtfully.

'No indeed,' Omo said. 'Full of vitamins!'

'Won't we have to cook them?'

'Yes, but the sun will do that for you. They aren't used to the sun. Lay them out on a hot rock and they'll soon be roasted.'

The roasted grubs were not half bad. In fact, with appetites made keen by two days of hunger, everyone voted them to be delicious.

'Where you found them there ought to be termites,' Omo said. 'They like rotten wood too.'

Omo's guess proved to be correct. In another part of the log the boys came upon a nest of termites, the so-called 'white ants'. They were big and plump. Hating the sun, they tried to escape into their tunnels in the wood. Hal and Roger scooped them out and placed them on a hot rock, in the blazing sun. They curled up, died, and fried.

Again the boys dined. They became almost merry.

Roger smacked his lips. 'I won't know what to do when I get home if I don't have my grubs and termites,' he said.

Further search revealed nothing. Just before the sun sank in the west Hal dived to bring up more drinking water. It seemed to him that the submarine stream was not quite as strong as it had been. It was perhaps caused by the rain that had fallen upon the island a few days before. This water filtering down through the rocks was coming out below. But it would not keep coming if there were no more rain. Rather anxiously, Hal returned to camp, but said nothing about his fears.

'Surely there must be some fish in these waters,' he said. 'How can we catch them?'

They debated the possibilities. It was a real problem since they had no fishline, no hook, no rod, no bait, no net, no spear.

Omo, if he had been his usual self, probably would have come up with the answer. But he was very tired and presently went to sleep. Hal and Roger continued to wrestle with the problem, but the younger brother was getting drowsy.

'We might make a trap,' Hal said, 'If we had a crate or a box or a basket.'

'But we haven't,' yawned Roger, 'so we don't make a trap.'

'Yes, we do!' cried Hal, and was out of the hut before he had finished the words. Roger sleepily followed, wondering what crazy idea possessed his brother now.

Though the sun had gone there was still some light in the sky. Hal trudged to the ocean shore where he began to fling rocks about.

'Will you tell me what you are up to?'

'We'll build a fish-trap of stone. Now's a good time – at low tide. We make a circular wall. When the tide rises it will fill with water and perhaps some fish will swim into it. When the tide goes down some of them may be left there, trapped.'

'Pretty neat, if it works,' agreed Roger, and they began to build the wall. They extended it a few feet into the sea so that even at low tide there would be a little water in the trap.

When it was finished the weir stood three feet high and was about twenty feet across.

Hal calculated that the tide would be high a little after midnight and low again at sunrise.

When the first rays of the sun felt their way into the sharkskin hut the next morning they found Roger awake and thinking about breakfast. His repast of grubs and termites had been long since digested and he was ready for something more substantial.

'Wake up, you dope! Let's see what's in our trap.'

In the shallow water at the bottom of the trap several finny creatures were dashing about seeking a way of escape. One of them was a gorgeous fish in a coat of green and gold with fine stripes of blue and red. Hal identified it as an angel fish. There were two other fish that were less beautiful but better eating – a young barracuda and a mullet.

Also there was a poisonous scorpion fish which they left in the pool hoping that the next tide would take it away.

Roger was about to lay hand on a cone-shaped starfish but Hal stopped him.

'There's poison in those barbs,' he said. 'If you puncture your hand on them your arm swells up and then your body and pretty soon your heart stops beating.'

Roger gave it a wide berth. They caught the fish with their hands and took them to camp. Omo was delighted.

'Of course we could eat them raw,' he said, 'but they'd taste a lot better cooked. If I had any strength in these arms I'd make a fire.'

'Let me try it,' Hal said, not too confidently for he remembered his troubles in producing a fire on the floating island in the Amazon.

First he must get tinder. That at least was easy. From the rotten log he scraped up a quantity of wood dust and split off chips and slivers. Then he and Roger accumulated a pile of bark and sticks cut from this and other logs.

'Now to find a firestick,' Hal said. 'It must be very white and dry.'

'How will this do?' Roger brought up a piece of driftwood from the shore. It was extremely light and dry as a bone.

'Just the thing!' said Hal.

He split off a little of it and whittled it to a sharp point. Then he braced the larger piece against a stone and began to rub it up and down with the point of the small stick.

His hands moved faster and faster. Only strength and great speed would bring success. Perspiration dripped from his face. The point was wearing a groove. The wood dust scraped off by it fell to the end of the groove.

Faster went the point. The groove began to smoke. Then a wisp of flame rose from the dust.

Roger, lying on his stomach, encouraged the flame by gently blowing upon it. It was now burning brightly. Hal stopped scraping to lay slivers of wood across the dust. These caught fire. Larger pieces were added. The fire was burning well.

'Phew!' exclaimed Hal, wiping his forehead. 'I think I prefer matches!'

The boys hurriedly and not too carefully cleaned the fish, then speared them on the ends of sticks and held them over the fire.

Breakfast that morning was a grand occasion. The merry castaways ate every scrap of the fish and washed it down with sparkling spring water. It was a delicious meal. Now they could forget the horrors of the first three days. They had conquered the desert island.

'At least we know now that we can hold out until Kaggs gets back,' Roger said, picking up a stick in which he had already made three notches. He began on a fourth notch.

'What's that for?' Hal inquired.

'Just to keep track of the days,' Roger said. 'You see, the stick is just long enough for fourteen notches. That's when I expect to see that old motor-boat chugging into this lagoon. Boy, won't that be a happy day!'

'It's time I told you a few things,' Hal said. 'I haven't told you before because we were pretty low and I didn't want to make you feel worse. We'll have to forget about Kaggs. We'd better start building a raft.'

Roger and Omo stared at him. 'A raft!' Roger protested. 'What's the use of that when there's a motor-boat?'

'The boat won't come back,' Hal said. He went on to tell them how he had altered the bearings so that Kaggs would not be able to find the island. 'So I'm afraid I gummed things up pretty badly.'

'You sure did!' agreed his younger brother indignantly.

'No, no,' Omo said gently. 'You did just what you had to do. It was the best thing to do. It means that Kaggs can't steal this pearl bed. You've saved the professor's experiment and perhaps some very valuable treasure. That was your duty to the man who employed you. As for us – we're not all that important. And anyhow, we'll get out of this. Luckily we have plenty of logs for building a raft.'

'But we have to have more than logs,' said Roger practically. 'How are we going to fasten them together without any nails, bolts, screws, or rope? And have you forgotten the job we were supposed to do for the professor? We were to get him some specimens of his pearls so that he could see how they were doing. And Omo is the only one of us who can dive that deep. And I'll bet a plugged nickel that Omo won't be doing any diving with that hole in his leg!'

'Then we'll have to do the diving,' Hal said.

Roger's jaw dropped. 'Sixty feet? When we've never done more than thirty? You're crazy!'

Hal grinned and said nothing. He knew his kid brother. After Roger finished saying that the thing was impossible, he would probably be the very one to do it.

Presently Roger slipped out. After a time, Hal followed. Sure enough, Roger was practising diving in the bay of pearls.

Roger came up, puffing and blowing.

When he was able to speak he said,

'I can't get below thirty. I wish I had a pair of lead boots to pull me down.'

'I'll run over to the store and get a pair for you. In the meantime you might use a rock.'

'That's right, so I could.'

Roger seized a rock twice as big as his head and slipped into the water. He went down rapidly at first, then more slowly, and finally reached the bottom. He held the rock under one arm and with the other pulled loose an oyster. Then he dropped the rock and rose to the surface. He laid the big brown shell on the shore.

Since he had not been down more than twenty seconds the changes in pressure had not greatly affected him.

'That was swell!' he chortled after he had caught his

breath. 'But it will take a year if we can only bring up one shell at a time.'

'If we could make a basket . . .'

'Out of what?'

'I don't know. Let's ask Omo.'

Omo, when consulted, sent them out to look at the heads of the fallen palm trees. He said they would find cloth and out of it they could make a bag.

'I think he's spoofing us,' Roger said.

But they found the 'cloth'. It was like a mat, a brown criss-cross of fibres formerly wrapped around the bases of the leaves.

It was a simple matter to cut out a sheet of it with their knives. They laced the edges together with some of the fibres so that the sheet was turned into a bag.

'And why can't we make shirts out of this stuff?' Hal wondered.

Roger's shirt had been used to collect the water and Hal's had been ripped up for use as bandages and a tourniquet. The tropical sun reflecting on the white rocks had badly burned their skin.

They made shirts. They were not quite of the latest fashionable cut but they served to filter the sun.

'And I want a pair of dark glasses,' Roger said. The eyes of both boys were bloodshot, thanks to the merciless glare. Hal had been worrying about this. Castaways on such unshaded reefs sometimes went blind. So he welcomed his brother's suggestion.

They made masks of the matting long enough to go around and tie behind the head. They could see through the weave as through coarse cheesecloth. Most of the sun glare was cut off.

'That feels a lot better,' Hal sighed.

'But I hope I don't look as funny as you do,' Roger laughed, inspecting his brother in his brown mask and the shirt that resembled a shaggy doormat. With no razor to keep them down, bristling black whiskers had sprouted on his cheeks and chin. 'You sure look like Blackbeard the Pirate.'

'Let's surprise Omo.'

The two masked bandits crept back to the hut and prowled into the dark interior. Omo who had been dozing looked up with a start and gave a cry of alarm – then he recognized his strange visitors. He admired the shirts, masks, and bag.

'I think you must be half Polynesian,' he said, 'you make such good use of what you find here.'

The two boys returned to the cove in high spirits. Omo's approval meant a good deal to them.

'I only hope we're good enough Polynesians to bring up some pearls,' Hal said.

But it was not too easy. Hal, after shedding his clothes, stepped in with the bag and a stone to carry him down. Reaching the bottom he quickly filled the bag with shell. But when he tried to rise with the bag he found it to be too heavy. He had to take out all but three shells before he could come up with it.

'What we need is a rope,' he said. 'We'd tie it to the bag. The man on the bottom could fill the bag and the man on top could haul it up. I think we'd better suspend operations until we can find some rope.'

'Guess you're right,' Roger agreed. 'We need it for the raft too – to fasten the logs together. But what chance have we got of finding rope on these rocks!'

They spent most of the day in the search. They learned from Omo that the Polynesians make rope from the husk of the coconut. But they had found only one nut and its husk wasn't enough to make even a ball of string.

A liana would do as a rope – but such stout vines did not grow on reefs.

On their Amazon journey, they had seen jungle Indians use strips of the skin of the boa-constrictor and of the anaconda as rope. But there were no snakes, large or small, on coral atolls. There were sometimes sea snakes in the lagoons. They could find none in this one.

But they did discover some much-needed food. They returned to camp in the evening with a cucumber, a cabbage, and a pint of milk!

'Won't Omo be surprised?' Roger chuckled. 'Who'd ever have thought that we'd find a vegetable garden and a cow on a coral reef!'

Omo gratefully drank some of the rich milk. He knew that the cow from which it had come was the coconut tree – not from a nut but from a flower stem. And the cabbage was a palm cabbage, the coconut bud resembling a head of cabbage or lettuce, but much better tasting.

The cucumber never grew in a vegetable garden. It was the sea cucumber or sea slug or bêche-de-mer, highly prized as a table delicacy by the Chinese.

They had found it on a coral shelf in the lagoon. It was shaped like a huge cucumber and had the same sort of a grooved or warty skin. It was a foot long but when they took it out it shrank to half that length.

Hal recognized it as the variety that is able to sting the flesh with its feelers and eject a poison that will cause blindness. So he did not touch it with his fingers but only with the point of his knife. He left it to die and dry in the sun while they went about their other errands.

After bringing it to camp, they cut it open under Omo's direction and stripped out the five long white muscles. These they broiled over a fire. They made a surprisingly good meal.

17 | The giant with ten arms

THE strange food gave Roger a nightmare. He squirmed and tossed, then woke with a start.

'The sea slug!' he screamed. 'My eyes! I'm blind! I'm blind!'

'Aw, shut up and go to sleep!' growled Hal.

But Roger was too disturbed to sleep. He crawled out of the hut. He was relieved to find that he was not blind.

The tree stumps rose around him like black statues.

The clock of the stars told him that it was about 3 a.m. The Southern Cross was reflected in the lagoon.

He walked along the beach of the lagoon, trying to calm himself. He was still all stirred up inside. He crossed to the ocean shore. The sea was silent. There was not a ripple. The tide was going down.

He idly wondered what had been caught in the trap. He walked to its edge and looked in.

Then he got the start of his life. Two great eyes looked back at him.

They were as big as dinner plates. Surely no living thing could have such great eyes. He must still be dreaming. This must be another nightmare.

The eyes glowed with a ghostly green light. They seemed to have lamps behind them. They looked like green traffic signals, but of enormous size. They said, 'Go!' and Roger felt like going, but his legs were so weak that he could scarcely move.

Suddenly the water in the pool shook as if agitated by some tremendous creature and the two circles of green flame came closer to Roger.

He let out a terrified yell, but still could not run. He was glued to the spot as if hypnotized. That was the way it was in a dream. He must be dreaming.

Hal came tumbling to his side. 'What's all the hollering about?' he demanded angrily. 'Why can't you let a fellow sleep?'

Then he saw what Roger saw. Like Roger, he could hardly believe that it was real.

'They look like eyes,' he said. 'They can't be. No eyes ever came that big. They must be little schools of phosphorescent plankton – little creatures that float on the surface.'

'You're nuts!' Roger blurted. 'Plankton don't swim in a circle. They're eyes, and nothing else. Gosh, they look as big as manholes.' He drew back as if afraid he would fall into the great green pools. 'Look out! It's coming!'

The Thing lurched towards them a foot or two, sending them back in a panic. Its movements splashed tons of water out of the pool. Great black twisting things like enormous snakes went up into the air and then fell back.

'A giant squid!' cried Hal. He approached to get a better look. Suddenly a great arm snaked out towards him. He jumped back just in time to escape it – but both he and Roger were soaked with spray.

'He's splashing sea water,' Roger said.

'No, he's squirting ink. We're covered with the stuff. Don't let it get into your eyes.'

They moved out of range.

Roger said, 'No wonder they call him the pen-and-ink fish!'

'Yes, and it's good ink. You can write with it. It's like Indian ink. I remember something about an explorer who wrote a page in his logbook with squid ink.'

'See him thrash about. Won't he come after us?'

'I don't think he'll come ashore.'

'But can't he escape into the sea?'

'He could easily enough if he knew how. But he's as

stupid as he is big. I don't suppose he's ever been in a spot like that before and he doesn't know what to make of it.'

'I wish we could take him alive. Mr Bassin wanted one of these.'

'He won't get this one. We can only hope we'll come up with another after we get back to our schooner. There are lots of them in the Humboldt Current.'

'That's the current that flows up the coast of South America and then out towards these islands?'

'Right. You remember that book we read about six young scientists on a balsa raft? They sailed from Peru to the islands on that current. They saw dozens of these things. They rise and float on the surface at night and sink down to great depths in the daytime.'

The huge green eyes burned now bright and now dim as if someone inside were turning the lights up and down. Roger shivered.

'Gosh, doesn't he ever wink?' He thought of the eight-armed monster he had wrestled with in the cave. Its eyes had been evil too, but small, and almost like human eyes. And they had not been phosphorescent like these. 'Now I begin to see the difference between a squid and an octopus. I've always wondered.'

'It's more than the difference between eyes like plates and eyes like thimbles. The body of the octopus is a bag; the squid is shaped like a torpedo. He looks something like a giant fountain pen, and acts like one. And he has ten tentacles instead of eight. Two of the tentacles are extra long. And the cups that line the tentacles are not suction cups. They are edged with sharp teeth and very dangerous. They can actually cut wire.'

'Aren't you putting it a little strong?'

'Not a bit of it. On an expedition of the American Museum of Natural History scientists had the light steel wire cables used as fish-line leaders cut in two by these tentacle teeth. So look out for them – unless you're made of something tougher than wire.'

As dawn came on and the darkness dissolved into grey light they could see the monster clearly. It completely filled the walled pool. In fact there was not room for its mighty arms, which lay sprawled over the rocks of the shore.

Its torpedo-shaped body kept changing colour – from black to brown, from brown to tan, from tan to sickly white.

The eyes were more than a foot across. They were even more terrifying than they had been at night. The green phosphorescence had faded out of them and they were now a deadly black like two dark caves out of which any horror might come. They were fixed upon Hal and Roger with savage hatred. The boys felt very small under that relentless unblinking gaze.

'Nightmare of the Pacific!' breathed Hal. 'He deserves his name!'

The tide had not entirely ebbed. But it had gone down enough so that there was very little water left in the rock-rimmed pool. The squid could easily have escaped while the tide was high. But, unaware of its danger, it had sunk as the tide ebbed until now it was locked between the rock walls.

The water was black with ink expelled by the angry prisoner. Now and then it filled its body with water and ejected it like a rocket, but only succeeded in ramming its rear against the wall.

'Look at the size of it!' marvelled Roger. 'It's twenty feet if it's an inch – just the body – and those longest tentacles make another twenty feet.'

'But it's really small as squids go. Specimens have been found with tentacles forty-two feet long. The fellows on one scientific expedition were lucky enough to see a battle between a giant squid and a sperm whale. The squid won. It was seventy-five feet long.'

'Well,' said Roger, 'this dainty little forty-foot item is plenty big enough for my money! Too bad we can't use him. I suppose he'll escape when the tide rises.'

'Perhaps we can use him!' exclaimed Hal. 'Didn't we need rope?'

'Rope! How can you get rope out of a squid?'

'Those tentacles. I'll bet they could be cut into strips that would be as tough as leather.'

Roger grunted his disbelief.

'Well, why not?' went on Hal. 'If they can do it with boaconstrictor or anaconda hide, why not with this? Down in Malaysia they use python skin. It's so durable they cover furniture with it and sell it in London shops. It's almost impossible to wear it out. And one of these tentacles is just as strong as any python or anaconda.'

'Perhaps so,' admitted Roger. 'I know I'd hate to be hugged by one. But you can't just walk up and help yourself to a tentacle – his honour might object.'

The sun had risen and its heat roused the monster to fury. The giant squid prefers the chill waters of the Arctic or Antarctic. It does not mind being carried from the Antarctic up into tropical seas by the Humboldt Current because that current is very cold. The squid stays in the chill depths of the current during the day. When the sun has gone it floats up to the surface but sinks when the sun returns. It is a rabid sun-hater.

The giant squid, trapped in the blazing heat, began to thrash about violently. Its tentacles flailed the rocks and their sharp teeth made deep scratches in the coral.

Suddenly with a mighty heave it lurched forward six feet and at the same time flung out one of its long tentacles. Roger fled to safety. Hal, trying to escape, stumbled and fell.

At once the great arm slipped around his waist. It tightened upon him. He could feel the teeth biting into him through his palm-cloth shirt.

Roger was beating the tentacle with a piece of coral and shouting, 'Omo! Omo!'

The tentacle began to draw Hal towards the monster's beak. The huge eagle-like beak opened, revealing a jagged row of teeth. Hal clung to the rocks with all his might but it was no use. The tentacle, as powerful as a python, pulled him loose. He clutched other rocks and again was pulled away.

Omo came hobbling on his two hands and his one good leg, dragging the other after him.

'Hurry, Omo!' yelled Roger. Somehow he had faith that the Polynesian would know what to do. Roger flung away his rock. It had made no impression upon the tentacle. Now he caught his brother's foot in both hands, braced himself behind a boulder, and held on like grim death.

But two boys and a boulder were no match for the giant. It dragged both of them and the stone as well. Now Hal was within a few feet of the waiting beak.

'Look out!' he gasped. Another tentacle was feeling for Roger, who squirmed to one side to avoid it.

Omo, arriving at last, picked up a large rock. Then he stood up, balancing himself on his good leg, and hurled the rock. Long training had made him as accurate with a stone as with a spear or a bow and arrow. Though he was weak from his illness, new strength came to him at this moment when he needed it most.

The rock flew straight into the monster's jaws where it jammed so tightly that the creature could not get rid of it.

With a mouthful of rock, the giant must abandon its notion of making a meal out of the castaways. But it could still punish with its tentacles and it proceeded to do so.

'Quick! Help me with this log!' Omo called. Roger dropped Hal's foot and gave Omo a hand in lifting a coconut log.

'Now! Ram it between the eyes.'

They ran forward with the log, Omo ignoring the excruciating pain in his leg, and crashed the end of the log into the monster's brain.

The squid threw up its arms in a violent spasm. Hal was lifted ten feet into the air, then dropped free upon the rocks.

The ten tentacles writhed and twisted as a snake does when in its death throes. Then the life went out of them and they lay still.

Roger and Omo turned to help Hal. But he was already on his feet. He was very unsteady. Where he had lain the coral was stained red. Blood flowed from the many cuts around his body.

'I'm okay,' he said. 'They're just scratches. Come on, Roger, let's give Omo a lift.'

They acted as two crutches, one under each arm, and got Omo back to the hut. There the Polynesian boy collapsed in pain and for the rest of that day had a pretty bad time of it.

Hal and Roger went back to the dead giant. The rock that Omo had thrown was still locked in the great beak. Hal shivered as he looked at the serpent-like tentacle that had held him in its crushing embrace. He still felt dazed by the shock and terror of those moments.

'I'm sorry we had to kill the beast,' he said. He had the naturalist's dislike for taking lives.

'It was either His Nibs or you,' Roger reminded him. 'Besides, we need his rope if we're going to get off this reef alive.'

'That's right. And we'd better get busy before the tide comes along and carries him off.'

The hide was like tough leather. It took many hours of hard work before the ten tentacles could be severed and laid out on the rocks to dry in the sun. 'Tomorrow we'll cut them into strips,' Hal said.

The tide had risen and was tugging at the body. 'Say goodbye to the carcass,' said Roger. 'Or would you like to have some of it for dinner?'

'I think I'll pass that up. The Orientals eat the young squids and find them very tasty, but I'd hate to tackle this old granddad. However, there's one more thing we need from it before we let the sea take it.'

With a block of coral he pounded the razor-sharp beak until a part of it broke off. It was like the blade of an axe. Then he cut out a stick from the flank of a coconut log. With a narrow strap cut from a tentacle he bound the blade to the handle.

'It may not be beautiful,' he said, swinging the jerry-built axe, 'but it will come in handy when we build that raft.'

18 | The pearl divers

THE next day narrow straps were cut from the tentacles of the giant squid. All flesh was scraped away from the inside surface. The straps quickly dried in the sun.

'Don't we need to tan them?' asked Roger.

'If we wanted them to last for years we would have to tan them. But it isn't necessary for our purposes. They will stand up all right for a few weeks.'

'It seems funny to be making leather out of squid tentacles.'

'Why so? They make leather out of other things just as strange – kangaroo, wallaby, buffalo, ostrich, deer, lizard, alligator, shark, seal, and walrus. Cannibals have even made leather out of human skin.'

By tying together the ends of the four straps they had cut from one of the twenty-foot tentacles they were able to get a line more than long enough to reach to the bottom of the cove. They fastened it to the palm-cloth bag and were ready for diving operations.

'Let me go first,' demanded Roger.

He tucked a rock under one arm, gripped the bag with his other hand, and dropped into the lagoon. The ripples he left on the surface gave Hal a wobbly vision of his brother as he descended to the floor of the bay.

Roger had difficulty in keeping his feet under him. They insisted upon floating upward. He stopped this by gripping the rock between his feet. That brought his feet down and head up.

The pressure upon his body was tremendous. He felt as if he were being hugged by a monster. It was all he could do to prevent the stored breath from popping out of his lungs.

He began tearing loose the big bivalves and putting them in the bag. The shells were rough and sometimes thorny. He was sorry he had not worn Omo's gloves. Bloody scratches appeared on his hand. If a shark got a whiff of that blood – but there were not likely to be sharks inside the lagoon. He hoped not anyhow.

It took about fifteen shells to fill the bag. He stuck it out until the job was finished. How long had he been in this terrific compression chamber? It seemed like half an hour.

He left the full bag on the bottom and rose to the surface. Hal gave him a hand and pulled him out onto the rocks. He breathed with sharp whistling gasps. He writhed in agony, cramps convulsing his body. His features were contorted with pain and the veins stood out on his face and arms. He shook in the hot sunshine as if he had the ague. He felt cold and weak.

Hal was anxiously scolding him.

'You stayed down too long. You were down two minutes. Even the Polynesians can't do more than three.'

Roger managed to sit up. 'I'm all right,' he said dizzily. 'Pull up the bag. Let's see what we got.'

Hal laid hold of the line and drew the bag to the surface. Before he took it out of the water he placed his arms beneath it lest the weight of the shell might break the palm cloth. He emptied the bag on the beach. Fifteen huge shells looking like so many black turtles lay before them.

They could not wait to see what they contained. They opened them one after another and explored for pearls. There were none.

Roger gazed into the depths of the cove with dismay.

'Don't tell me we have to go through that again!'

'Many times, I'm afraid. Now it's my turn.'

'Wear the gloves,' Roger advised him, looking at his own red hand. 'It will save you some blood.'

Hal put on the gloves, provided himself with a rock and the bag, and went down. He spent no time trying to bring

his feet under him but let them float upward like sea fans while he hastily filled the bag.

Then he came up, trying to make the ascent as slow as possible. But when Roger had helped him out he lay on the shelf of rock completely exhausted, with drops of blood trickling from his ears, nose, and mouth. His chest rose and fell like a bellows as he breathed in great gulps of the good air.

'I'm afraid I'm no – amphibian,' he panted.

Roger hauled up the bag and they eagerly opened the shells.

They worked alternately, Roger opening the first shell, Hal the second, and so on. Twelve shells were opened without result. The next one fell to Roger.

'Thirteen!' he grumbled. 'There can't be any good luck in that one!'

He thrust his knife into the muscle, twisted it, and the lips of the shell eased apart. He ran his finger along the inside rim of the lower lip.

He stopped half-way. He looked up at Hal and his eyes became round and his mouth dropped open. He began to breathe fast.

'Golly, I believe this is it!'

His fingers closed upon it. He brought it out. For a moment neither could speak. They sat stunned, gazing at it.

Then Hal whispered, 'Holy Moses! It's as big as a barn!'

It was not as big as a barn, but it *was* as big as a marble. It was the largest pearl the boys had ever laid eyes upon. It was a perfect sphere. Held in one position it seemed white, in another its opalescent depths reflected all the colours of lagoon and sky. It seemed alive.

Roger dropped it in Hal's hand. Hal was surprised to find it so heavy. That meant it was a good pearl. He turned it slowly in his fingers. It did not have a single flaw or blemish. It was so unreal, so full of a mysterious light, that it seemed to be part of the sunshine or of the atmosphere.

When he cupped his other hand over it to shade it from the sun, it still glowed, but now like a moon.

Roger, a dazed expression on his face, murmured, 'Boy! Wait till the prof sees that!'

'I think he'll decide that his experiment has been a success!'

'A success, and how! But it's a long way from here to the professor. Suppose we lose it. Or have it stolen. That Kaggs will be watching for us when we get back to Ponape – if we ever get there.'

'Quit worrying!' laughed Hal. But it was plain he also felt the great responsibility that had been suddenly thrust upon them. 'That's the trouble with treasure,' he said. 'Once you get it, you have to start worrying about keeping it. Let's show it to Omo.'

Inside the dark cave the pearl still gleamed as if it had a fire of its own. Hal held it before Omo's eyes. Omo whistled softly.

'It's the finest pearl I've ever seen,' he said. 'We never get them that big in these waters. Your professor has certainly proved how a Persian Gulf oyster can make itself at home in the Pacific! Hand me that cup of water.'

He dropped the pearl into the coconut shell full of water. It sank swiftly to the bottom. 'That shows its weight is excellent.'

'Keep it for us,' Hal said. 'I'm scared to death for fear I might drop it. It will be safe with you. You take care of it.'

'Not on your life!' exclaimed Omo. 'It would keep me awake nights. I'm afraid you're stuck with it.'

Hal reluctantly took the pearl, wrapped it in palm fibre to increase its bulk so that it would be less likely to be dropped unnoticed, and put it in the pocket of his dungarees. He felt as if it at once began burning a hole. Now he had something to be anxious about, day and night.

'Well,' he sighed, 'we may as well get back to work. The professor will want more than one specimen to judge by.'

Before the day ended two more pearls had been wrapped in with the first. The second was a shade smaller, the third a bit larger. Together they represented what Omo called 'a comfortable fortune'.

'*Un*comfortable, I'd say!' snorted Hal. 'I know I won't be comfortable until I deliver these dratted things to Professor Richard Stuyvesant!'

And in a troubled sleep he dreamed that the raft upset, and sank deep into the ocean, and a shark pulled off his dungarees. Then he saw that the shark was really Kaggs with an evil grin on his face and three pearls in his hand.

He woke in a sweat and clutched his pocket. The precious package was still there.

19 | The raft

THE raft was built on a sand beach sloping down towards the lagoon.

Impulsive Roger began to haul logs at once. But cautious Hal, with his habit of looking ahead, foresaw that the raft when built would be too heavy for two boys to carry to the water's edge.

He placed one log near the shore and parallel to it, and another a little farther back. These were not to be part of the raft but would serve as rollers. The raft would be built on top of them and, when finished, could be easily rolled into the lagoon.

Seven logs fifteen to twenty feet long were laid side by side upon the rollers. The longest ones were placed in the middle to make a sort of bow. Logs that were too long had to be reduced to the right length. It could not have been done without the help of the beak-bladed axe.

The seven logs were lashed together with squid-hide straps.

The boys stood back and inspected their work.

'It begins to look shipshape,' Hal said. 'But we ought to have a cabin to protect us from the sun. And we should have a sail.'

Roger laughed mirthlessly and looked about him at the coral rocks. 'Not much material for either one,' he remarked. 'But wait a minute. How about that roof?' He was looking at the hut. 'We could get a cabin roof out of that.'

'And a sail too!' exclaimed Hal. Then his face fell. 'But what do we do for a mast? A palm log would be too big.'

The answer to this problem meant more hard work. With

stone wedges hammered into a log by means of coral blocks, they split the log in two. After splitting again, and once again, they had a stake about eighteen feet long and four inches through. With their knives they shaped it until it was nearly round.

It was rough and crooked and would have brought shame to any shipyard, but the boys were proud of it.

They whittled and hacked until they had made a hole in the raft near the bow, and in this hole they stepped their mast.

The cabin and sails must wait until they had no more need for their hut.

The building of the raft took the best part of three days. More days were consumed in gathering supplies for the voyage.

The most important supply was water. They must get it at once or there would be none to be had, for the undersea spring was failing steadily. Several times a day they had been diving for water, bringing up each time a coconut shell full. And every time the stream was weaker and the water more brackish.

Hal consulted Omo.

'How are we going to carry water on the raft? One shellful would be no use, and we can't find any more coconuts.'

Omo knit his brows. 'That's a hard one. On our island we had goats and we could make a water bag out of goatskin. Perhaps if a dolphin stumbled into your trap you could use its skin.'

'But we can't wait for perhapses. We've got to store some water now before it stops flowing.'

Omo returned to his whittling. He was skilful with a knife and had already made himself a pair of crutches out of coconut wood. Now, from thin slabs of wood that the others had split from a coconut log, he was fashioning paddles for use on the raft. He looked at the half-shaped paddle before him.

'We do almost everything with coconut. It feeds, shelters, and clothes us. I suppose you could even make a water cask out of a section of it, but it would be hard. You would have to hollow it out . . .'

'Hold on!' cried Hal. 'How about using something that is already hollowed out?'

Omo looked at him with a puzzled air.

'On the other island,' went on Hal, 'we found a clump of bamboo. Of course it had been blown down by the storm, but —'

'Just the thing! Cut it into lengths about six feet long.'

But when this had been done there was a new difficulty.

Three bamboo logs were cut, each about five inches in diameter. They were hollow – but not quite!

At every joint the hollow chamber was closed by a stout partition.

How could these be broken down? Only the first one could be reached with the knife.

A swordfish came to the rescue. It had been caught in the trap two days before, and its excellent meat had provided many fine meals.

It was Roger who thought of calling upon the swordfish for help in the present emergency. He slipped away to the shore near the trap where the skeleton lay.

Dropping upon it a huge block of coral almost as heavy as himself, he broke off the sword. It was three feet long and came to a hard sharp point. He increased its length by lashing it to a stick.

Now he had a formidable spear. He knew that this spear would break much more than a bamboo partition. The swordfish has been known to ram its sword through the stout hulls of boats. One in Palau lagoon pierced not only the hull of a motor-boat but the metal petrol tank, letting out the petrol and setting the boat adrift.

Hal was delighted with his brother's ingenuity. Both gripping the spear, they rammed it down into one of the bamboo tubes. They broke one partition after another until all were gone except the one that closed the bottom end of the tube.

When the three tubes had all been treated in this way they carried them to the shore just above the submarine spring. They took turns in diving with the coconut shell, bringing up water and emptying it into the tubes. It was an all-day job. When the tubes were full they corked them with plugs of coconut wood. They carried them to the raft, laid them in the dips between the logs, and lashed them in place.

'Now whatever else happens, we won't go thirsty,' Hal rejoiced.

The bamboo clump yielded some very useful by-products. Bamboo shoots were growing up from the roots. They had evidently begun since the storm. Omo explained that this was not surprising – bamboo grows very rapidly, sometimes as much as a foot a day. The shoots added a much-needed vegetable to the diet of the castaways.

Also the bamboo gave them sugar! A sweet juice coming from the joints hardened into a white substance that Omo called Indian honey. It was almost like toffee and made a very pleasant dessert.

'Imagine finding candy on a desert island!' mumbled Roger, with his mouth full of the sweet gum.

The bamboo also gave them a cooking-pot. A single section of bamboo was used for this purpose. Water could be boiled in it without any fear of burning the pot.

Another bamboo trunk was prepared for the storage of food.

They cut fish into strips and dried it in the sun. (How it smelled while drying!) It should be salted too, but they were at a loss to know how to get salt until Omo told them how it was done in the islands. Sea water placed in a hollowed rock was allowed to evaporate. When it was gone a thin film of salt was left.

As for the oysters they had brought up from the cove of

pearls, they ate as many as they could, but had little luck in preserving them for future use. However, they packed a few untasty morsels of oyster into the bamboo tube along with the sun-dried salted fish.

Into the bamboo went also some dried seaweed of the sort considered good food by the Orientals. Roger was not enthusiastic about it.

'Looks like spinach to me,' he grumbled. 'And tastes worse.'

A few birds had returned to the island, among them that comic creature known as a megapode. It flew as sluggishly as a cargo plane and waddled when it walked over the rocks. Evidently it had not learned to be afraid of human beings. It came running when Omo knocked two stones together. For some strange reason this sound had an irresistible attraction for the comedian.

Omo caught it easily and after it was dressed and cooked it was added to the store.

Sea urchins containing masses of eggs went into the tube. The eggs were edible but one had to be careful not to be stuck by the spines which, in this variety, carried a poison like a cobra's.

One night Roger was awakened by scratching in the beach. He crawled out of the hut in time to see what looked like a round dark boulder crawling towards the water's edge. It was a sea turtle, two hundred pounds of fine food. It had probably come ashore to lay its eggs in the sand, and that explained the scratching Roger had heard.

He could not allow it to escape into the lagoon. He ran after it and fell upon its back. It did not seem to mind and continued its march. Roger dug his feet into the sand, but was dragged loose.

He jumped off the back, seized the edge of the shell, and tried to turn the big fellow over. It was too much for him. He called for help.

Before Hal and Omo could get the sleep out of their eyes,

the turtle had reached the lagoon and plunged in.

But Roger was not ready to quit. He swung himself on board the turtle's back as on a horse. He knew how Polynesian boys ride turtles, though he had never tried it himself.

He gripped the front of the shell just back of the leathery neck. Then he threw his weight backwards and pulled up.

That prevented the turtle from diving. It was forced to swim on the surface.

But it kept straight on going out into the lagoon, headed for the pass and the ocean. Roger tried to remember what he should do next. Oh yes, he must get hold of one of those hind flippers.

He reached back with one hand and got the right hind flipper. He held it tightly so that it could not paddle.

With the other three flippers going and this one quiet, the turtle could not help going around to the right. Roger held on until headed back towards the beach, then let go.

He could dimly see Hal and Omo on the beach.

'I'm bringing home the bacon,' he called to them.

But the turtle had ideas of its own. It began to swing one way and then the other and Roger was kept busy seizing the right or the left hind flipper to keep his course straight for the beach. When he forgot to hold back on the front edge of the shell the creature promptly sounded and Roger was carried a fathom or so under water before he could collect his wits and bring his submarine back to the surface.

Hal and Omo waded into the water and helped him get his mount ashore. The big turtle snapped its jaws together and nearly nipped a piece out of Hal's leg.

'We'll soon stop that,' said Hal, and took out his knife.

The turtle raised its head menacingly. Its leathery skin and appearance of great age made it look like an angry old man.

'Don't murder grandpa!' cried Roger. 'I've a better idea. Let's take him along with us on the raft – alive. Then we'll have fresh food when we need it.'

'Good idea,' said Omo. He was digging in the sand with a stick. 'But it's grandma, not grandpa. Here are the eggs she was laying.'

In a pit a foot deep the turtle had buried more than a hundred eggs.

Roger was surprised, upon picking one up, to find that it was soft like a rubber ball. It did not have a brittle shell like a hen's egg.

'How do you eat it?'

'You bite a hole in the skin, then squeeze the insides into your mouth. They're good food. We'll boil them and take them along.'

Grandma was tethered to a stump and the boys turned in. At dawn they were stirring.

They agreed that they had enough supplies. Today they would take off on their hazardous voyage.

They took down the sharkskin that had served them as a roof and cut it in two. It made two sections, each eight by ten feet. One would make the sail, the other the cabin.

A rough spar was lashed to the upper edge of the sail and it was then hoisted to the masthead by squid-leather halyards. To each of the lower corners of the sharkskin sail was attached a line by which it could be sheeted home.

The cabin was a simple affair. Three split bamboo canes were curved to form the framework, their ends fastened to the deck. Over them was laid the sharkskin with its two edges touching the deck and lashed fast to the logs.

The result was a shelter that looked something like half a barrel. It was precisely like the roof of a Chinese sampan except that it was made of sharkskin instead of matting.

'It's just like the *toldo* we had on our boat on the Amazon,' Roger said.

It was, except that it was lower and snugger, which was a good thing in case of a Pacific storm. It was only three feet high and five feet wide. From front to back it measured

eight feet. It was quite large enough to lie in and furnished
protection from the tropical sun. Since the front and rear
ends of it were open, the man at stern paddle could look
straight through to the bow.

The turtle eggs were boiled and stored. Grandma was led
on board and lashed to the mast.

Now that they were ready to go, they began to regret
leaving the spot that had been home to them for two event-
ful weeks. They did not need to be told of the dangers of an
ocean voyage on a raft.

They would be at the mercy of wind and wave. They
would try to go south, but might just as easily be driven
north, east, or west. Their paddles and crude sail would be
of small consequence compared with the force of wind and
current.

They tried to cover their fears by shouting and singing as
they made preparations for casting off.

'Let me christen her,' cried Roger. Lacking a bottle of
champagne, he smashed a turtle egg on the bow log and
proclaimed, 'I christen thee the good ship *Hope*!'

Then the three mariners rolled the craft into the lagoon
and hopped aboard.

The momentum of the launching carried the raft across
the bay of pearls. Hal and Omo studied its behaviour carefully.

'It floats high and dry,' Omo said.

'And it holds its course well,' Hal remarked. Thanks to
the pointed bow, and the straightness and smoothness of
the coconut logs, the vessel showed no tendency to yaw
over to starboard or port. 'How does she answer the helm?'

Omo at stern paddle put his weight on the blade and the
vessel veered slowly to starboard.

'It does pretty well for a raft.'

The wind was on the beam and Hal trimmed the great
rectangle of sharkskin sail to take advantage of it.

But to get through the pass it was necessary to go

straight into the wind's eye. Rather than trouble to lower the sail for the few moments necessary to make the passage, Roger sheeted it so that it was edge on into the wind.

Then the boys took to their paddles. It was a stiff job, but Hal had estimated correctly that the ebbing tide would help them escape from the lagoon in spite of the wind. After fifteen sweating minutes they were in the clear, and the home-made *Hope* rose and fell on the swells of the greatest of oceans.

20 | Disaster in the waterspout

THE first two days of the voyage passed so smoothly that the mariners three almost forgot the anxiety with which they had begun the trip.

The wind held from the north-east and they sailed steadily south. If this kept up, they should reach Ponape, or, failing that, they would at least get into the shipping lane that runs from the Marshall Islands to Kusaie, Ponape, Truk, and Yap. There they might hail some schooner that would pick them up.

By day the sun was their compass and by night the stars. They roughly divided the twenty-four hours into twelve watches so that no man had to stick at the steering paddle for more than two hours at a time. Although they had no chronometer, they could compute time with a fair degree of accuracy by the angle of the sun or a star above the horizon.

Water sloshing up through the cracks between the logs kept them a bit wet all the time, but the dampness was cool and pleasant. When one began to suffer from the blows of the equatorial sun he had only to crawl into the cabin and lie in the cool shade of the sharkskin roof.

The bamboo tubes of drinking water nestling between the logs were kept cool by the water that splashed up from beneath. Hal was a trifle worried because the food seemed to be disappearing rather fast, but he hoped they would be able to catch some fish.

Brilliantly coloured dolphins played alongside. They were usually bright blue and green and their fins were golden yellow. But they could change colour like a chameleon and sometimes they shone like burnished copper. One flopped on board and as it died it lost its colour and became silver grey with black spots.

On the third day a big whale investigated the *Hope*. It came straight for the raft, blowing and puffing each time its great head reared up out of the water. It seemed strange to hear heavy breathing in these fishy wastes where breathing was not the fashion – except for the boys on the raft; and they almost stopped breathing at the thought of what a sixty-foot monster could do to a few logs.

'Just one flick of that tail,' worried Roger, 'and we'd be in the drink.'

The whale circled the raft twice. Then he dived and up-ended his tail twenty feet into the air, carrying with it a huge quantity of water that fell like a heavy shower upon the voyagers.

The tail went down with a violent twist that sent a great wave of water across the raft from stem to stern, drenching its occupants.

'Ring up the plumber!' cried Roger, standing in water up to his knees.

But the raft had one great advantage over a boat. The water simply ran out through the floor.

The whale went under the raft and came up on the other side so close that another wave was rolled over the vessel. The beast's shoulder crashed into the starboard logs and it seemed for a moment that the good ship *Hope* would be turning into kindling wood.

As if satisfied with the scare he had given these intruders in his domain, the whale sounded and was seen no more.

The outside log with its lashings torn loose was about to float away. The boys recovered it just in time and tied it fast.

During the morning the wind failed and the heavy shark-skin sail thudded idly against the mast. The swells lost their rough finish and seemed as smooth as oil. Without a breeze, the sun seemed ten times as hot.

Omo looked about. 'I don't like it,' he said. 'A sudden calm like this may mean trouble.'

But there was no cloud in the sky. The only thing visible was a dark column like a pillar far to the east.

Presently, a few miles farther north, another appeared.

'Waterspouts,' Omo said. 'There are more of them in this part of the Pacific than anywhere else in the world.'

'Are they dangerous?'

'Some are, some aren't. Those two aren't. They're something like the dust whirls on land – you've seen them. They carry papers and leaves several hundred feet high. "Dust devils", you call them. But —' and he scanned the horizon anxiously, 'those little fellows are often just a sign that a big one is coming. And a big one is like a tornado. In fact, that's just what it is, a sea tornado.'

'But a land tornado can carry off houses!' said Hal.

'Exactly,' replied Omo. 'And I am afraid you are soon going to find out what a sea tornado can do.' He was looking up at a point a little north-east of the zenith.

The others followed his gaze.

A cloud formed before their eyes. It seemed to be about three thousand feet up. It became rapidly blacker and blacker and squirmed violently so that it looked like a living monster. A long tail dangled from it.

No wonder, thought Hal, that the Polynesians call it a sky beast and have many superstitions about it.

Greenish lights that one might imagine were eyes gleamed in the writhing blackness.

'It can't be as bad as the hurricane we had,' Roger said.

'It can be worse,' Omo replied. 'Of course it won't last as long. And it isn't as big. A hurricane can be six hundred miles across but these things are never more than two or three thousand feet. But it makes up in violence what it lacks in size. I'd choose a hurricane any day.'

Hal was itching to do something. 'Can't we get out of

here? Do we just sit here and wait for it to grab us?' He dug his paddle into the water.

'You may as well save your strength,' Omo said. 'You can never tell which way the thing will go. We might paddle straight into it. The only thing we can do is to hold on and hope.'

The tail of the monster grew longer every moment. Now it looked like a long black tentacle groping towards the sea like the arm of an octopus.

The air had been breathlessly quiet, and still was around the raft. But from the cloud came a roaring or a rushing sound such as you hear when you paddle down a river towards a waterfall.

Now something was happening to the sea beneath that groping tentacle. The oily surface broke up into sharp ridges. Spurts of spray began to race round and round like elves in a wild dance.

The spinning became more intense. Now masses of water were joining the mad whirl, carried around by a screaming wind.

And yet there was not the breath of a breeze on the raft.

Hal knew that the land tornado acts in the same way. It may pick up one house and carry it away and not disturb another ten feet off. He had heard of a tornado that tore the roof from a house and yet did not budge a tin top resting on a churn outside the back door.

'It may skip us,' he said.

'Perhaps.' But Omo did not sound too hopeful.

'Shall we take down the sail?'

'If it wants the sail it will take it, no matter whether it is down or up.'

It was agonizing to know that you were completely at the mercy of the monster and there was not a thing you could do about it.

The spinning water had now become a great whirlpool. But instead of a hole in the centre of the whirlpool, there was a hill. There the sea was bulging upwards. It climbed higher and higher as if drawn from above. Now it rose to a conical point higher than the *Hope*'s masthead.

The whirling cone threw off spray and loose water that acted most strangely. Instead of falling to the sea it climbed into the sky, turning into a rapidly revolving ghost of mist.

The tentacle reached lower, the arm of the sea reached higher. They met and joined with a loud hiss.

Now it was truly something to see, that great spinning pillar three thousand feet high. At the top it spread out into the black cloud and at the bottom it spread again to take in the whirlpool. The whirlpool was a frightful thing to behold, a crazy merry-go-round of wild horses racing to the shrill organ music of the wind. The swirling maelstrom covered more and more of the sea. Now the storm circle was two thousand feet across.

Within the circle the waves rose to points and crashed together as if determined to beat each other's brains out.

'Bet that wind is travelling two hundred miles an hour,' shouted Hal. But the roar of wind and water was so great that he could not be heard.

The lofty column began to lean as if the upper end were being pushed. Hal breathed a sigh of relief as he saw that it was leaning away from the raft. Those upper winds were carrying the sky beast southwards and the *Hope* would escape its fury.

But the waterspout is a fickle giant and loves to tantalize its victims. The leaning tower changed direction, swayed one way and then another, writhed and twisted like a fabulous boa-constrictor hanging from a branch of heaven.

A seagull drifting placidly through the quiet sunny air was suddenly snatched by the whirlwind and tossed upwards, spinning round and round, its wings beating helplessly, until it was swallowed by the sky beast above.

What made everything go up? Even at a moment of peril such as this, Hal's scientific mind asked questions and

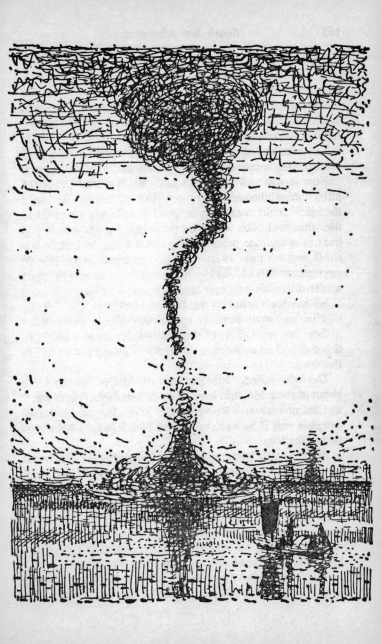

figured out the answers.

The air rushed upwards to fill a low-pressure area above. It whirled, for the same reason that hurricanes whirl, for the same reason that ordinary winds are inclined to travel in circles, because of the rotation of the earth. The centrifugal force of this whirling made almost a vacuum inside the column and therefore the sea was sucked up. In a land tornado that vacuum around a house made the walls burst out because the air pressure was so much greater inside the house than outside. Corks pop out of bottles during a tornado for the same reason. And it suddenly occurred to him that if the storm caught the raft the plugs would pop out of the bamboo tubes and the water would be lost.

He had no time to consider this problem, much less do anything to solve it. Suddenly a giant finger of wind slipped under the cabin roof and carried it up and away. The boys threw themselves flat on the deck and held on.

The sail went next. It spun away like a crazy thing around the great circle of the whirlwind, rose to a height of a hundred feet or more, and then was tossed out to fall in the sea.

Daylight faded. The air seemed full of water. Omo shouted something but his voice was inaudible. There was a deafening roar and Roger would have clapped his palms over his ears if he had not needed both hands to hold himself to the logs.

Now the raft was caught in the frantic circle. The waves stood up in spear points, then crashed their tons of water down upon the raft and its passengers. At times the *Hope* was completely buried. Then it would leap up into the air through a smother of foam. The boys held on as if to the backs of bucking broncos.

Grandma was the first to go. A wave flicked her off and broke her leash. She was tossed a dozen yards, whirling like a top, before she disappeared into the flank of another wave.

Hal could look into the side of the wave as into a store window. He saw grandma turn tail up and swim straight down to the depths where all would be calm and peaceful.

You could do worse than copy a wise old turtle. He resolved to do the same thing if the raft broke up.

The hill of water at the heart of the waterspout crept now closer, now farther away, keeping the sailors trembling between hope and despair.

The boys could not look steadily at anything. Their eyes were beaten shut by the wind.

With so much air flying past them, still it was difficult to get enough to breathe. You dared not face the wind – it would ram its way down your nose and throat and fill you like a balloon. If you turned your head away you were in a vacuum where there was no air to be had. You must bury your face between the logs, or protect your nose and mouth with your hand, in order to slow up the air long enough to get some of it into the lungs.

And just when you had found a way to do it, you would be buried under tons of water. Sometimes it seemed that you would never come up.

As the raft rose to the surface after one of these plunges, Hal saw that the whirling hill was bearing down upon them. It looked like a moving volcano, the black column rising from it resembling smoke. The entire column was leaning now, with its top passing over the raft. Hal thought it was like a tree – but ten times as high as the loftiest giant sequoia in California.

As the spinning hill approached, the wind changed its tactics. Instead of blowing sideways, it blew up. Now they were coming into the heart of the updraught.

On land, it was strong enough to carry up roofs and heavy timbers. Would it lift the raft, crew and all, and carry them high into the sky like Arabian Nights' passengers on a magic carpet?

More likely it would break up the raft and beat them to

death with the thrashing logs. That was why they should swim down.

Hal put his mouth close to Roger's ear.

'Swim down!' he shouted.

The updraught was already tugging at their bodies. What was left of their palm-cloth shirts was now ripped loose and carried up the black pipe as through a pneumatic tube in a department store until it reached the cloud above.

If the hill would only stop coming, the centrifugal force might throw the raft away from it. Hal tried to believe that this would happen. If faith could move mountains, perhaps faith could stop a mountain from moving.

But the gods of the winds far above were deciding where the hill should go. They took a malicious delight in carrying it down upon the raft.

Suddenly the forlorn *Hope* faced a solid wall of green water. High up in this glassy wall, far above the raft, Hal was horrified to see a large shark. There it was like a stuffed specimen in a glass case.

He had only a glimpse of it before the raft upended on the flank of the hill and the tumultuous waters writhing under the suck of the tornado wrenched the logs apart as if they had been matches tied with fine thread.

A moment more and those tossing logs might brain them. Hal knew that Omo would know what to do – but he clung to his log until he was sure of Roger. When he saw that both boys had dived straight down, he did the same.

It was not easy to swim down for the water was running uphill, twisting and tossing him, pushing him back where the sky beast might suck him up through its trunk as a butterfly sucks a drop of honey from a flower.

He put all his power into his stroke. Now the pressure upwards was less and he could begin to swim out.

He stayed beneath the surface turmoil. It did not matter what direction he took so long as he swam straight. Any direction would take him to the edge of the circle.

The eternal quiet below was very soothing. After the frenzied tumult above he could almost rest as he swam. He was conscious of some current even at a depth of a couple of fathoms but he knew that this current was centrifugal and would help carry him out. This whirlpool, unlike most, whirled out instead of in.

When his wind was spent he surfaced, only to find himself still within the whirl. He submerged and swam on. When he came up again he found himself among small choppy waves beyond the reach of the tornado.

The column was leaning more than ever and the entire spout was travelling towards the south-west. The circle of clashing waves, with the Tower of Babel in the centre, slid away across the sea and the scream of the winds diminished.

The air around Hal was now as quiet as it had been before the sky monster's arrival. The clashing waves gradually settled down.

It was not until then that Hal thought of the shark. He wondered if it also had been terrified by the commotion. Now that the commotion was over, would it begin to take an interest in him and his companions?

He saw a brown head break surface a hundred feet away.

'Hi there, Omo!' he called. 'How's tricks?'

'Glad you're okay, Hal,' shouted Omo. 'Have you seen Roger?'

'No. Suppose you circle around one way and I'll go the other.'

They swam in opposite directions around the recently troubled area. Hal wondered how the younger boy had stood the experience. Would the kid be so scared stiff that he couldn't swim? Had he lost his head, come to the surface, and been bashed to death by flying logs?

He did not need to worry. When he found Roger, the boy was not only safe, but busy. He had discovered two logs and had towed one alongside the other. Now he was trying to lash them together with the broken pieces of squidskin strap that hung from the logs.

'Good work!' shouted Hal. 'I'll see if I can find some more logs.'

Omo joined the search. They swam back and forth across the circle where the raft had broken up and as far out into the sea in all directions as they dared, but found no more logs. They must be somewhere, but lay so low that it was difficult to spot them from any distance.

There was a blast of thunder. Lightning blazed in the black cloud that topped the waterspout. Thunder rolled again.

Then the great squirming hose that connected sky and sea broke in the middle. The lower part collapsed, causing gigantic waves. The higher portion coiled up into the cloud.

Bombs seemed to be exploding in the cloud. Then a heavy rain fell from it. The upper winds quickened and the thundercloud, with the rainstorm that hung from it like a trailing dress, travelled swiftly towards the horizon.

The sky monster was gone, but it left three badly discouraged boys behind it. Hal and Omo searched in vain for more fragments of the lost *Hope*.

Wearily, they returned to the two logs. They crawled aboard and lay down. Three men were too much for the slender raft and it began to sink.

Roger slid off into the water and held on by one hand. The raft rose until the top was about level with the surface. Every wave rolled over it and over the bodies that lay upon it.

The bamboo tubes of food and water were gone. The mariners were without sail or paddles, without shelter, without even palm-cloth shirts and eye-masks to protect them from the whipping sun, without enough of a craft to support all three of them at one time, without weapons except their knives in case of attack from below.

Roger, submerged up to his neck, kept glancing furtively

about, expecting the dorsal fin of a shark to break surface at any moment.

'I don't know about you guys,' he said, 'but I'm a-feelin' mighty low!'

Omo, whose face had been twisted with pain by too vigorous use of his lame leg, raised his head and smiled.

'I'm rested now,' he said. 'Let's change.'

He slipped into the water and Roger took his place on the logs.

'It's not so bad,' Omo said softly. 'We're all alive. We've got two logs, three pairs of dungarees, and three knives. And we still have some pearls to deliver – or have we?'

Hal clapped his hand to his pocket. 'We have!'

'Good. So we'd better set about delivering them.'

He slipped around to the end of the logs and began to swim, pushing the raft before him. He headed it south. Slowly it ploughed through the ripples.

Perhaps it didn't help much, but it was a lot better than doing nothing. Hal's heart was filled with deep affection for his Polynesian friend. So long as there was such courage and patience aboard, the *Hope* was not lost after all.

21 | The wreck of the 'Hope'

THEY took turns overboard. After lying on the hard logs for an hour or so with the waves breaking in your face, it was a relief to swim and push for a while and get the kinks out of your muscles.

And after swimming a while it was a relief to climb aboard and stretch out.

But as time went on each relief grew less and there was nothing but continual discomfort.

Night was especially hard to bear. It was impossible to sleep. You must be continually awake and alert, ready to hold your breath when a wave swept over. You no sooner dozed than you awoke half-strangled by water pouring into nose and mouth.

Dozens of strange and somewhat terrifying creatures came up to investigate this floating thing. The boys had never seen the ocean so full of life.

It is always full of life but the passenger on a schooner or steamer sees little of it. A few dolphins and flying-fish may come near, but most denizens of the deep are afraid to approach the monstrous moving thing with smoke billowing from its funnels or sails beating the sky.

Even seven logs with cabin and sail are much more frightening than two logs, mostly submerged. This little floating affair might be just a strange fish, and the other fish came to call.

The depths below were full of travelling lights like a city at night seen from the sky. Roger looked down over the edge of the raft.

'There goes a lantern fish. And there's a star-eater. Gosh, what's that?'

Two enormous eyes were lazily following the raft. They were more than a foot wide and they shone with a yellow-green light.

'That's your old friend, the giant squid,' Hal said.

Roger shivered. 'He's no friend of mine! Couldn't he reach up and grab us?'

'He could. But it isn't a pleasant thought, so let's not entertain it.'

And Hal who was serving as the ship's engine at the moment put some extra power into his stroke and the two eyes were left behind.

But something far more startling now appeared. It seemed like another eye, but huge, not an inch less than eight feet across. It glowed with a silvery light. It came up on the starboard bow and moved slowly along with the raft about a fathom down. It looked like the full moon.

Roger was speechless. It wasn't often that Roger could find nothing to say. Omo put his hand on the boy's arm and found that he was trembling.

And who would not tremble when followed by a monster big enough to have an eye of such a size!

'It's not an eye this time,' Omo said. 'It's a moonfish – called that because it shines like the moon and it's round.'

'A round fish? Are you kidding me?'

'No. What you're looking at is its head.'

'Then where's the rest of it?'

'There isn't any rest. It's nothing but head. So some people call it the headfish. And it has one more name. Sunfish – because it lies asleep on the surface in the daytime and basks in the sun.'

'Doesn't it ever have anything more than a head?'

'When it's young, yes. But it loses its tail, the way a tadpole does. Of course the head is really something more than a head because it has a stomach in it and other organs. And those little fluttering things on the edge are fins.'

The fins seemed very small to propel such a big bulk.

'It must weigh close to a ton,' Roger marvelled.

'They do. Sometimes we amuse ourselves by stepping out of our canoes upon a sleeping sunfish, pretending it's an island.'

The underwater moon travelled along with the raft for several minutes. Then Roger's blood chilled as four great snakelike creatures swam over the light. They had no phosphoresence of their own and their twisting bodies were blackly silhouetted against the glow of the moonfish. They were from eight to ten feet long and as thick as a man's leg.

'Are they snakes?'

'Morays,' Omo said, and he drew his knife. 'A kind of eel. Watch out for them. They will eat anything – including us.'

'Mean customers!' Hal said, splashing to keep off attackers. 'Who was that old Roman we read about in school who kept a tankful of pet morays? He used to feed them by tossing in a slave every morning.'

Omo was peering intently into the water, knife in hand. 'We call this kind *Kamichic*, the Terrible One. It's amphibious. It can even climb a mangrove tree and wait to pounce upon any prey passing below. While we were in Ponape a man was bitten by one and taken to the hospital.

He died after two days.'

The serpentine forms passed back and forth beneath the raft. Roger too had his knife ready.

'But would they come aboard the raft?'

'They might. Sometimes one of them boards a boat. It gets a grip on the gunwale with its tail, then flips its body in. Most animals won't attack unless they're bothered, but the moray is always spoiling for a fight. It has teeth an inch long and as sharp as the point of this knife.'

Roger gripped his knife. 'The first one that shows itself will get its head lopped off.'

'That would be the worst thing you could do,' Omo warned him. 'The blood would bring the sharks. Besides, their heads and necks are very tough – but their tails are tender. They can't stand being rapped on the tail.'

Roger, lying on his side and looking down, felt a touch on his back.

Before he could turn Omo reached forward and brought the heavy handle of his knife down hard.

'That one won't bother us any more!'

Almost in Roger's face a black tail slipped over the log, gripped fast, and powerful muscles flung a writhing figure up out of the sea. Against the stars Roger had a glimpse of an evil head and open jaws coming his way. But at the same instant his knife handle was thudding down upon the tail. A contortion twisted the eel's body and it fell into the water.

There were no more snaky forms to be seen against the submarine moon.

Roger felt dizzy and weak. He had as much spunk as any boy of his age, but this night was a bit too thick for him. He immediately feel asleep, but was as promptly aroused when water buried his face.

Omo saw that if the boy did not get some sleep he would crack.

'Sit up, Roger.' The boy obeyed. 'Now turn around with

your back to me. All right – now just relax and go to sleep.'

Roger was too weary to argue. Supported in a sitting position by Omo he let his head drop upon the Polynesian's shoulder and was instantly asleep. Now the waves rarely reached high enough to touch his face. When they did, Omo put his hand over the boy's nose and mouth. When it was Omo's turn to go overboard, Hal took his place. The change did not wake Roger.

The rising wind chilled the wet bodies of the castaways. They were glad to see the sun rise. But it had not been up for an hour before they began to long for the cool of the night.

Roger woke, refreshed by his sleep, but hungry and thirsty. He was indignant because he had been the only one to get any sleep.

'What the heck!' he fumed. 'If you guys can take it, I can. I don't need a baby-sitter.'

He looked at his companions' hands and then at his own. They were shrivelled and wrinkled by the salt water.

'We look like a pack o' mummies! Pass the cold cream.'

There being no cold cream available, he slipped over the side and took Hal's place as motor of the not very good ship *Hope*.

Thirst and hunger became more acute as the day wore on. Constant immersion in the water had one good feature – moisture was absorbed through the pores, and the moisture of the body could not be so rapidly evaporated, so that thirst crawled up on them more slowly than on land. But by night they would have given one of the pearls, if it had been theirs to give, for a long drink of fresh water.

During this night Roger insisted upon being baby-sitter for his companions, taking them alternately. He could hardly keep his eyes open. Once he did drop off and he and Hal, whom he was supporting, both rolled over into the sea. The cold plunge brought them smartly back to their senses.

The next morning found a school of bonito swimming

about the raft. The boys repeatedly plunged their hands into the sea but failed to catch any of them.

'Wonder if we could make a fishline?' Omo was examining the bark on the logs. 'We usually make it from the husk of the nut. But bark might do.'

They spent most of the day picking out fibres from the bark, twisting and braiding them into a line. It was only five feet long when finished, but fairly strong. Omo gouged a splinter from a log and carved a hook. There was nothing to put on it for bait.

They dangled the hook in the water and hoped. Would any fish be fool enough to swallow a bare hook?

The school of bonito had disappeared. There were other fish, but they paid no attention to the hook.

Another night and another day. Sores began to appear on the boys' bodies due to salt water and chafing of the skin against the logs. Their feet were swollen and tingling and spotted with blotchy red areas and blisters.

'It's "immersion foot",' Hal said, and added gloomily, 'Salt-water boils will come next.'

Their skins, constantly wet and salted, were being severely burned by the sun. Their eyes were bloodshot, inflamed and painful.

Thirst cracked the lips. The tongue swelled until it seemed that there was hardly room for it inside the mouth. It kept trying to push its way out between the lips, like the end of a wedge. The whole inside of the mouth felt as if smeared with glue. Roger rinsed his mouth with sea water, and swallowed a little.

'Go easy with that,' Hal warned him. 'A very little won't hurt. But it's hard to stop with a little.'

'Everybody needs salt,' objected Roger. 'What could it do to you?'

'Too much will put you in a coma. Then you have two chances. You may come out of it crazy, or not come out at all.'

'What's the difference?' Roger said bitterly. 'We'll get the purple moo-moo whether we drink sea water or not.' He passed his hand over his forehead. 'I'm beginning to see things already – things that aren't there.'

'Such as what?'

'Such as a rainstorm. Cool, sweet rain falling! Over there.' He pointed to the south-east. 'I know it can't be, but ...'

'But it is!' cried Hal. Not half a mile away a small shower was streaking down and spattering the sea. 'Let's go!'

They tumbled overboard and joined Omo behind the raft. All three pushing, they propelled the logs rapidly towards the spot.

But before they could reach it they were sorely disappointed to see the rain fade into mist and the mist dissolve in sunshine.

'Look! There's another one!' This time it was only a quarter-mile west. Surely they could reach it in time. The water fell from a small black cloud that was being carried west by a light breeze.

They swam with all their strength. They soon saw that it was hopeless. They tired, but the breeze did not tire. The harder they swam, the farther away the shower seemed to be.

Presently the little cloud rained itself out and there was no sign that there had ever been a shower.

'Do you think we just imagined it?' Roger said doubtfully.

'Of course not. We all saw it, didn't we?' No one answered. 'Well, didn't we? Didn't you see it, Omo?'

'I think so,' Omo hesitated. 'I – I'm not sure of anything any more.'

'Well, here's something we can be sure of!' cried Roger. 'Because I've got my hands on it. An albacore has swallowed our hook.' He lifted the fish for them to see. It was black and glossy, not more than a foot and a half long, but plump with good meat.

They attacked it at once with their knives and devoured everything but the bones – and one scrap which they saved to bait the hook.

They felt better – and not so thirsty. The flesh of a fish, specially a juicy one like the albacore, contains moisture – and it is fresh water, not salt. But it was not enough. It hardly amounted to a tablespoonful for each man.

The baited hook worked better than the bare one and soon attracted a young sawfish. It was hauled aboard and quickly eaten, saving only enough for bait.

Where there are young sawfish there are apt to be larger ones and Hal was not surprised to see sudden turmoil in the water.

'Look out!' he cried to Omo who was swimming. A huge sawfish was wildly dashing about attacking small fish with its great saw. After slashing them to bits it would feed upon the torn flesh. The sawfish was sixteen feet long and could cut a man in two as easily as a fish. Many a whale has been attacked by a sawfish, and the whale has not always been the winner.

Omo did his best to keep out of the way of the great blade. The mangled bodies of the small fish rose to the surface and Hal and Roger seized as many of them as they could get their hands on.

Attracted by the blood, a huge tiger shark hove in view. It darted at some of the torn fish and gulped them down.

This annoyed the sawfish, which came at once to the attack. It did not plunge its weapon straight into the shark as a swordfish would have done. It came within six feet, then swung its saw with a sidelong movement and slashed deep into the body of the shark. Blood poured out.

'There'll be a hundred sharks here in ten minutes,' Hal cried. 'This is no place for us.'

He slid overboard and Roger followed suit. Their legs

tingled with dread of the savage saw.

They joined Omo and quickly pushed the raft away from the scene of slaughter. Looking back, they saw the sea boil with the thrashing of many sharks and turn red with their blood.

They munched tattered shreds of fish.

'That sawfish did us a good turn,' said Hal. 'You see, not *all* the luck is against us.'

But on the following day the luck ran pretty thin. The only fish that came near were jellyfish. They covered the sea thickly for miles. The man behind swam through them and the two on deck were washed by them every time a wave went over. The stinging tentacles of the jellyfish, which are powerful enough to paralyse fishes, were like nettles on the boys' skins.

The worst of the jellyfish was the 'sea blubber', a red jellyfish that reaches a breadth of seven feet and has tentacles a hundred feet long. When the swimmer became tangled in the tentacles of one of these he had to call upon his companions to help unwind the stinging threads from his body.

Even after the *Hope* had made its way out of the sea of jellyfish the logs were still covered with a slippery stinging coat of jelly.

On the next day the first birds were seen. Noddies and boobies sailed inquisitively around the raft.

'It means that land isn't far away,' Omo said.

Sore eyes followed the horizon around but could not discover a single palm.

All three of the boys were now 'raft happy'. Or, as Roger had put it, they had 'the purple moo-moo'. They were sick of everything, even of each other.

Hal announced that he was tired of having Roger on the same raft with him. Roger retorted that he suffered most from not having anything to throw at Hal.

Each began to think the others were losing their minds.

They said strange things. Omo began to talk in his island language. He talked on and on. Roger said, 'I'm going up the beach'. He rose and started to walk off into the sea. Hal caught him by the ankle and brought him down with a thump.

Hal saw rainstorms – rainstorms that weren't there – and islands with palm trees and waterfalls tumbling from high cliffs through tropical forests soaked with spray.

So they hardly knew it when the wind quickened, the sky darkened, and the sea rose. Rain fell. They had barely enough wit left to raise their mouths to it.

An angry sea flung the raft south-westward. By a sort of desperate instinct, they clung to the logs.

The darkness of the storm merged into the darkness of night. Hal was vaguely conscious of the screaming wind and the sickening lift and drop of the raft over steep waves.

Then there was a roar that was not exactly the roar of the sea. It was the roar of a shore.

It must be another of his crazy fancies. It sounded like surf pounding upon land but it might be only the hammers in his aching head.

The raft was speeding forward dizzily now, only to be sucked back, then driven forward again. There was another surge, and a grinding sound underneath. Then another lift, and a crash.

The logs broke apart. There was no more motion. Hal felt hard sand under his body.

He reached for Roger. The boy had been thrown free of the surf.

But how about Omo? Omo had been in the water with his wrist secured under the lashing of the raft so that if he became unconscious he would not be lost. The lashing must now be broken, for the logs had parted.

Hal explored. The stars were blotted out by the storm and he could see nothing.

He groped all about the logs, then ventured back into the

surf. His foot struck something and he reached down. It was Omo. Hal pulled him out of the surf and ten feet up onto the beach.

Omo was as heavy as a sack of meal. He must be half-drowned.

Hal knew what he had to do. Take the pulse. Get the water out. Apply artificial respiration.

Hal dreamed he was doing all these things. But he had dropped upon the sand and was sound asleep.

22 | Rescue and rest

HAL woke in heaven. A golden-brown angel with red hibiscus flowers in her dark hair was holding a coconut shell full of cool sweet water to his lips.

It was hard to get any of it past his great tongue but he managed to swallow a little.

The sun had risen but was not beating upon him. He lay in the shade of stately coconut palms richly loaded with fruit. A soft breeze brought him the scent of flowers. There was music somewhere.

Roger and Omo lay beside him. Other golden-brown angels were ministering to them. Handsome young men came through the grove.

But he was very weak and closed his eyes. Now he was back in the storm and the night, clinging to the logs. He was conscious of being carried, but whether it was the waves that were carrying him he did not know.

Very gently he was laid down. There were many voices. He smelled wood smoke and the heavenly odour of cooking food.

He opened his eyes. He and his companions lay on clean mats in a sort of lanai or veranda in a village of thatch houses. Flowering vines clambered over the roofs. Above the houses stretched the protective arms of magnificent mango trees from which hung ripe orange-coloured fruits like ornaments on a Christmas tree.

At the edge of the veranda brown faces were peering in – gentle, friendly faces – not the faces of night and storm.

Someone was bending over him. It was his angel again. He smiled up at her. She fed him something from a wooden bowl with a wooden spoon. It was a sort of mush made of

breadfruit, bananas, and coconut milk and he thought it the
most divine food that had ever passed his lips.

When he choked she drew back, thinking she was feeding
him too fast. But it was gratitude, not his thick tongue, that
choked him.

An old man seated himself on the mat beside him. To
Hal's surprise, he spoke English.

'Garapan is my name. I am chief of this village. You
have had much suffering. Now you are among friends. You
will eat, drink and rest.'

Hal tried to say something but sleep closed over him like
a cloud.

When he woke the shadows were long. It must be late
afternoon. His eyes roved over the peaceful village. There
was no street; the houses were scattered among the trees.

And what trees! He had noticed the mango trees before.
Now he picked out breadfruit, banana, orange, lemon,
coconut, fig, papaya, and mulberry trees. All of them were
heavy with fruit.

Orchids of many colours clung to the trunks and
branches. Bougainvillaea, hibiscus, and convolvulus were
in bloom.

There were moving colours too – the red-and-green of
flitting parakeets, the rose-grey of doves, the metallic blue
of kingfishers. And there were tame little birds that flut-
tered around doorways as if they were the familiar friends
of the people inside. On their tiny coats nature had found
room for six colours – red, green, black, white, blue, and
yellow.

The whole wood gave out a contented chuckle of bird
sounds. Mingled with this music was the soft murmur of
voices in the thatch houses, and, from somewhere, singing
to the accompaniment of guitars.

He turned towards Roger and Omo. They were awake
and sitting up, entranced as he was by sight and sound.

Roger expressed it as usual in noble prose.

'Boy oh boy!' he murmured. 'Isn't this the cat's!'

'Let's not pinch ourselves,' Hal said. 'We might wake up and find it isn't true.'

There was a chatter of voices inside the house. Then several girls and women came out with shells of water and bowls of food which they placed before the castaways – baked fish and yams, roast pigeon, creamy poi, and a great basket of fruit of more than a dozen varieties.

The chief came to sit with them as they ate. His kindly old face beamed.

'Where are we?' asked Hal.

'This is Ruac. One of the islands of Truk.'

Truk, the paradise of the South seas! Hal had heard much about it. It was a vast lagoon surrounded by a reef one hundred and forty miles long. Within the lagoon were two hundred and forty-five islands.

'Is this island inside the lagoon?'

'No, it is on the reef. The ocean is yonder, and the lagoon is on the other side.'

'Are there any navy men here?'

'On the main island, yes. I went there this morning to report. They wished to come to see you at once. But I asked permission to care for you until tomorrow morning. They said you were reported missing from Ponape. If you wish, they will put you aboard the U.S.S. *Whidbey* which leaves tomorrow for Ponape and the Marshalls. It is a hospital ship – you will have good care.' He smiled. 'I have said what I was told to say. Now I shall speak for myself. We wish you to stay with us for many, many days and let us be your father and mother, your brothers and sisters.'

Hal could hardly keep back the tears.

'We can never forget your kindness,' he said. 'But we must go. We have much important business in Ponape.'

The next morning an outrigger canoe bore the derelicts across the fabulous lagoon of Truk. The lagoon was circular and forty miles across. Upon every side rose lovely islands, dozens upon dozens of them. Some of them stood up like towers and minarets, clothed from sea to summit with breadfruit and banana trees, coconut palms, scarlet bougainvillaea and crimson hibiscus, brilliant against the deep blue South Sea sky.

Some islands sloped up gently from sand beaches. Others rose abruptly in steep cliffs. Five of the islands climbed to peaks more than a thousand feet high.

Some islands were large. Tol was ten miles long, Moer five miles. Dublon, headquarters for the navy, was three miles across. There were islands of all sizes, down to half an acre or less.

And below, what a pageant! The lagoon floor was a garden of coral and algae, of sea fan and oarweed, of bright blue sea moss and red sea cucumbers, of ultra-marine starfish and of swimming fish in all the colours of the rainbow. There were corals like sponges and sponges like corals. There were green sponges, geranium-scarlet sponges, marigold-yellow sponges.

'It wouldn't annoy me to stay around here and sail on this lagoon for ever,' Hal remarked.

But an hour later on the U.S.S. *Whidbey* they sailed out of the lagoon through North-east Pass and looked back regretfully to the lovely island of Ruac. They could see their friends on the beach waving to the departing steamer.

Hal climbed to the bridge and spoke to Commander Bob Terence.

'Would you mind whistling good-bye to those people?'

The commander grinned and opened the whistle valve in three long blasts of farewell.

The *Whidbey* was a floating hospital. It was equipped with an X-ray, a fluoroscope, a pharmacy, and laboratory. Its business was to cruise from island to island, healing the sick and training native nurses.

Of most interest to the boys were cool clean beds with

white sheets. They did little but rest and eat. A skilful naval doctor treated their salt-water sores and sunburn. He pronounced Omo's wound to be nearly healed.

When Hal thought of Kaggs whose bullet had caused Omo so much suffering and who had left them all to live or die on a barren reef, his blood boiled and he could hardly wait to get his hands on the murderous pearl trader.

'I'll thrash him to within an inch of his life!' he vowed.

The commander radioed Ponape that the boys had been found and were coming on the *Whidbey*.

After three days of peaceful sailing the great Rock of Chokach was sighted and the *Whidbey* steamed into the island-studded harbour of Ponape. No sooner had the anchor been dropped than a launch came alongside and Commander Tom Brady and other officers climbed aboard.

Brady searched out Hal at once and began to ply him with questions.

'Where were you? What happened? What made you stay on the reef? Why didn't you come back in the boat?'

Hal laughed. 'One thing at a time. In the first place – did Kaggs come back?'

'Kaggs? Who's Kaggs?'

'Oh, I forgot. You know him as the Reverend Archibald Jones.'

'Jones was picked up by a fishing boat. He was stark staring mad. He had lost his way. His provisions and water had run out and he had been drinking sea water. It made him as crazy as a loon. It was days before we could get any sense out of him. We asked him about you. He said you had decided to stay on the island until he got back.'

'That wasn't quite the way of it,' Hal put in. 'He shot Omo, then abandoned us without provisions and skipped off in the boat. We could die there for all he cared. He wasn't a missionary – he's a pearl trader and his name is Merlin Kaggs. There's a bed of pearls up there and he's out to steal it.'

Brady stared. 'I always thought there was something screwy about his missionary talk.'

'Is he here now?'

'No. He got a larger boat and some men and sailed again. We thought he was going to get you. So imagine our surprise when we got word you were wrecked on Truk.'

'How long has he been gone?'

'About a week. He wouldn't say when he was coming back. He talked wild – claimed he was going to dig up the pot of gold at the end of the rainbow. He was still ninety per cent nuts. The men were almost afraid to go with him, he acted so strangely. He went about with a logbook clutched to his chest and wouldn't let anybody look in it. Began to foam at the mouth if anyone so much as touched it. He wouldn't tell us where he was going. Said it was a secret island and he had the bearings. He took along a native who has had training in navigation. So he'll get there all right.'

'He'll never get there,' Hal said. Brady looked at him inquiringly but Hal did not explain his remark. 'I hope he comes back soon. He'll find me waiting for him with a meat axe.'

Brady grinned. 'I know how you feel, but go easy with the meat axe. There's a prison sentence waiting for the Reverend Archibald Jones.'

But both Hal and Brady were wrong. Kaggs would escape the meat axe and he was not to go to prison. Something rather worse had already happened to him.

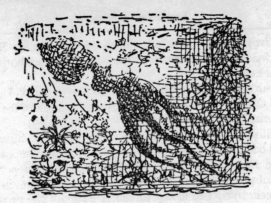

23 | Towards new adventures

THE boys moved in with Captain Ike in the same house to which they had been assigned when they had first come to Ponape. The captain reported that the repairs on the *Lively Lady* had been completed.

'She's shipshape and rarin' to go.'

'And how are the animals?'

'All in fine fettle. In fact, the octopus was feeling a bit too frisky. He got out of his tank and climbed the rigging. I had to call in a gang of natives to help me get him back in his tank.'

Hal sent a long radiogram to his father. And on the first plane flying east he dispatched a small but heavily insured package addressed to Professor Richard Stuyvesant.

He breathed more easily when the pearls were at last out of his hands.

Hal inquired about Crab, the young sailor who had tried to steal his secret and who had been clapped in jail for likkering up the natives. Crab was still in jail. Hal thought that he had been punished enough. He went to see Brady who, as deputy governor of the island, had authority to release the prisoner.

Crab was set free. He did not bother to thank Hal or Brady, but lost no time in signing on as a sailor on the next ship out.

Hal waited anxiously for some word of Kaggs. Since the pearl trader had the wrong bearings it should be impossible for him to find Pearl Lagoon. Should be. But suppose he had found it in spite of all! Suppose his men were even now at work diving in the bay of pearls. Suppose Kaggs wiped the bay clean of all its precious store. Then he would sail away with the treasure. He would not come back to Ponape.

Not finding the boys on the reef, nor their skeletons, he would guess that they had escaped and might have returned to Ponape. So he would give Ponape a wide berth. He would sail away with his fortune to parts unknown.

And then what could Hal say to Professor Richard Stuyvesant? He would have to admit that it was his fault. He had been fooled by the crook, had even taken him along as a passenger to the secret island! Imagine taking in a thief and showing him just where your money was hidden!

'What a dope I was!' The words drummed in Hal's mind over and over as he tossed sleeplessly on the Japanese mats of the house above the harbour.

When the sun rose he went down to the docks. A strange craft was just dropping anchor a hundred yards out. Several brown men and one white stepped into a dinghy and rowed towards shore.

Hal strained his eyes. Was he only hoping it, or was it true? The white man was Kaggs!

Hal's heart began to beat like a trip-hammer. Now would come the reckoning. Kaggs must answer now for his evil tricks.

The pearl trader doubtless toted a gun. Hal had no gun. He did wear a knife, but had no intention of using it. His

fists would have to do. He was seventy pounds lighter than
the trader and several inches shorter. Never mind – a tiger
is smaller than an elephant, but the tiger wins. He felt the
muscles tensing like steel wires in his arms.

Kaggs stepped out on the dock. He walked unsteadily.
His mouth hung open and his eyes stared. His unshaved
black beard increased his wild appearance. His uncombed
hair hung like a mat around his ears. The hunch in his back
was more pronounced. He looked like a deformed giant.
His great arms hung like cargo booms from his forward-
thrust shoulders.

Hal stood in his way. Kaggs stopped.

'Hello, Kaggs,' Hal said. 'Remember me?'

Hal expected to see a hand slip up to the shoulder holster
where he knew Kaggs carried his gun. Before it got half-
way Hal would strike first. He would land a crashing blow
on that wobbly jaw and another in the solar plexus.

But the big fellow's arms continued to hang. He stared
vacantly at Hal. Failing to recognize him, he turned out of
his way and staggered off along the dock, muttering mean-
ingless words as he went.

One of the men from the boat had stopped beside Hal.
He held a sextant in his hand. He must be the navigator.

'Completely out of his head,' he said, looking after Kaggs.

'What happened?' Hal asked.

'The crazy fool had some bearings in a logbook. He said
they were the bearings of an island where there was a
fortune in pearls. When we got to the position there was no
island there at all. He was already badly touched in the
head, but that made it worse. He just cracked to pieces. He
wanted to hunt for the island but we had had enough of
sailing around with a raving maniac hunting for islands
that don't exist. We brought him back.'

There was a commotion at the shore end of the dock and
Hal turned to see the cause of it. Kaggs was roaring and
struggling in the grip of two military police. He was led

away, babbling vacantly. Hal could almost feel sorry for the devil who had left him and his companions to die on a Pacific reef.

Kaggs was taken not to jail, but to the hospital. On an early plane he would be deported to San Francisco, there to be consigned to a mental institution.

Hal told himself that he should be happy over the way things had worked out. He had a good collection of specimens to take home, the pearling venture had been successful, their lives had been saved, and their enemy defeated.

But he felt strangely let down. He had not had the pleasure of punching Kaggs in the jaw. He could not take any delight in the terrible punishment the sea had meted out to his enemy. He shuddered to think how near he and Roger and Omo had come to losing their minds during the drift of the ill-fated raft. He would not wish such a fate upon anybody.

But he had another reason for low spirits. The great adventure was over. When he was on the island or on the raft he would have given anything to be done with it all. But now that it was all done, he was lost. He felt like an employee who has just been fired from his job. Nobody needed him any more. He was being laid on the shelf.

It was too bad that he must turn his back upon the South Seas. He had seen just enough of its wonders to want to see more.

And what gave him most pain was that he would have to part with Omo. Omo had already been looking about for a schooner headed for his home island of Raiatea.

Hal knew that Omo was as sad as he himself was over the coming separation. Roger, Omo, Hal, they were three brothers, and it was a pity to have to break up their alliance.

Gloomily, he walked up into the town. He stopped at the radio station. There was a radiogram for him. He opened it eagerly. It was from his father.

He read it with growing excitement. Then he broke out of the office and ran all the way to the house.

He found Roger, Omo, and Captain Ike each sitting in his own corner, moping. No one was saying anything. The place was as sad as a tomb.

'Great news, boys!' Hal shouted. 'I got a radiogram from Dad.'

'I'll bet I know what's in it,' Roger said. 'He tells us to toddle straight home.'

Hal did not answer. He began to read the message:

You have done a great job. Animal collection sounds fine. Ship it home on cargo steamer. Stuyvesant pronounces pearls superb and has warmest praise for your work. Come home if you have had enough.

'What did I tell you?' Roger interjected. 'We nearly break ourselves apart doing their job for them and then, just when we can begin to enjoy things, we have to quit!'

'Wait a minute,' Hal said. 'There's more to it.' And he read on:

If you wish to stay there is an opening for you and your ship with expedition of Scripps Oceanographic Institution now sailing from San Diego. Could meet you at Honolulu. They would outfit *Lively Lady* with diving-bell, diving-suits, nets, submarine cameras, etc., for deep-sea diving operations to study habits of great fish and capture specimens. If interested let me know and will air-mail you all particulars. Your mother sends love to you and most affectionate gratitude to your friend Omo.

Omo looked up and his eyes were filled with a warm happy light. He tried to speak but his voice choked.

'Golly, boys!' cried Captain Ike gleefully. 'That means we hang together!'

Roger began to leap about the room to the great peril of the Japanese paper doors.

'Whee! Whoopee! Meet the deep-sea divers! I'm going to be the first one down in the diving-bell!'

Hal smiled. 'It seems to be unanimously agreed that our answer is yes. I'll get a message off to Dad at once.'

But since what happened thereafter is another story, it is told in the pages of another book of this series, *Underwater Adventure*.

WILLARD PRICE

DIVING ADVENTURE

A Willard Price Adventure story, about Hal and Roger and their amazing adventures in search of wild animals for the world's zoos.

Hal and Roger go to stay in Undersea City, two hundred feet beneath the Great Barrier Reef of Australia. Travelling round in their glass jeep they find some strange and alarming creatures – the Floating Death, the whale-shark, the lionfish, giant sea snakes – and have some amazing adventures. Last but not least, there is hidden treasure. . .

MORE HIGH ADVENTURE STORIES
FROM KNIGHT BOOKS

WILLARD PRICE

☐	16303 8	Amazon Adventure	£1.95
☐	03993 0	Underwater Adventure	£1.95
☐	17217 7	Volcano Adventure	£1.95
☐	17218 5	Whale Adventure	£1.75
☐	14904 3	African Adventure	£1.95
☐	04243 5	Elephant Adventure	£1.95
☐	13500 X	Safari Adventure	£1.95
☐	10435 X	Lion Adventure	£1.95
☐	14903 5	Gorilla Adventure	£1.75
☐	16302 X	Diving Adventure	£1.75
☐	18272 5	Cannibal Adventure	£1.95
☐	25393 2	Tiger Adventure	£1.95
☐	26806 9	Arctic Adventure	£1.95